The Diary of Murder

Mysteries from the Antique Store

Sydney Tate

CAR Publishing

Contents

1. Chapter One   1

2. Chapter Two   7

3. Chapter Three   14

4. Chapter Four   22

5. Chapter Five   30

6. Chapter Six   39

7. Chapter Seven   45

8. Chapter Eight   49

9. Chapter Nine   59

10. Chapter Ten   72

11. Chapter Eleven   81

12. Chapter Twelve   91

13. Chapter Thirteen   96

14. Chapter Fourteen   106

15.	Chapter Fifteen	111
16.	Chapter Sixteen	122
17.	Chapter Seventeen	135
18.	Chapter Eighteen	149
19.	Chapter Nineteen	158
20.	Chapter Twenty	167
21.	Chapter Twenty-One	178
22.	Chapter Twenty-Two	180
Epilogue		189
Also by		192
About the author		195

Chapter One

August 21, 2023

Monday

"I don't like this." I squirm in my seat. I'm in the back of Em's, behind Jasper and his long legs driving.

Em twists around in her passenger seat to shoot me a warning glare. "You don't even know what *this* is."

"I don't have to know it to know I don't like it. Why does he want to bring someone to our lunch?" I chew my lip for a split second, then add, "I don't like it."

Em groans and Jasper makes an amused noise.

"What?" He's not even off my naughty lists after his stunt with Maura. So he better tread lightly.

"I'm just happy your mood will be pointed at someone besides me now."

He's lucky I barely acknowledge his words. I'm too busy worrying. "What if Maura has an even *more* evil twin?"

Now Jasper groans. "She's not evil. And you two grew up together. You'd know if she had a twin. You're being ri-" He stops himself from finishing that sentence, something else he's lucky for.

The car stops and I steel myself for whatever's about to happen. How can I stare down murderers—on the regular now, I might add—and still be terrified of lunch at Waldo's? I take another deep breath, telling myself that no matter what happens, at least I'll get some chicken tenders out of the deal.

Ugh, I wonder if Chase is gonna eat his stinky fish in front of this mystery date.

Is it a date? With us? Is this like a 'meet the parents' ambush?

Em taps on the window. "Get out, weirdo." Her phone buzzes and she makes a face that's not good or bad.

"What? If you leave me here with-"

She opens the door because I still haven't. "You've got five minutes to chill out and act like a grownup. They're at the light."

Reluctantly, I get out of the car and look over my shoulder toward the light he's stuck at, as if I can see through the trees and traffic, and into his car. Then I turn back and grab my phone.

Nothing.

"Are you in on it?" I ask Em.

"You know, Juniper Caine, this private eye stuff has made you so cynical." She throws an arm over my shoulder as we head inside to take our seats.

"It's also made me notice more things, like when suspects don't answer the question you asked them." I raise an eyebrow at her.

She glides into the one circular booth in the whole restaurant. "Oh, so I'm a suspect now?"

"TBD."

Jasper laughs and scoots all the way to the middle to make room for us. This booth is the coveted spot at Waldo's, so that it's just sitting open, waiting for us, puts Waldo on my suspect list, too.

"I don't like this."

Em gives me a straight line smile. "So you've said."

Somewhere inside myself, a five-minute alarm goes off, and I glance toward the door in time to see Chase walk in. For a brief, hopeful moment, I think he's alone, and this was all some horrible prank.

Then he steps aside and takes the hand of a petite brunette.

I gasp and jump up.

"Rebecca!" I run to them and wrap my arms around her. "You sly dog! How long have you been keeping this a secret?"

She blushes and hugs me tighter. "It wasn't my idea. I think this big oaf is kinda scared of you."

I let go of her and try to make a stern face at Chase, but it spreads into a wide grin. "As he should be." I hug him, too, and usher them toward the table.

Chase slides in beside Jasper, who's staring at me with his eyes narrowed.

"This is so unfair."

"What?" I ask.

"You've been plotting my death since you found out about Maura, but Chase hides a girlfriend for...how long?" He turns to Chase with his eyebrows raised.

"Four months."

My mouth drops open, but I don't get the chance to speak because Jasper's on a roll. "Four months! Your best friend-"

"Hey!" Em interrupts him with an elbow jab.

"Your second-best friend-"

"Hey!" Chase says, mocking Em's bruised ego tone.

Jasper groans. "You know what I mean! You've been hiding a girl-friend for four entire months and everything's fine."

I smile at Rebecca over the table. "Rebecca's not an evil corporate shark who made my life miserable for decades. She's nice and sweet and...perfect for Chase. Probably too good for him, really."

Rebecca smiles back and pats Chase's shoulder. "That's exactly what I say. Although having a big, strong man around is kinda nice."

Chase picks up his napkin and fluffs it across his lap. "Kinda nice? Ouch."

Waldo comes up with a tray of drinks, sweet tea for me and Rebecca, coffee for Em, and waters for Chase and Jasper. It's comforting how well he knows all of us. "So, the usuals all around?" He beams at us and adds. "Gotta say I'm glad to finally see this."

"Me, too," Chase says.

Now for the real test. "I'm getting my usual," I say to Waldo, but really the whole table, and even more really, to Chase. Throwing down the gauntlet.

Em, Jasper, and Rebecca nod, but I barely see it because I'm staring straight at Chase.

He grins and raises his eyebrows at me. "Me, too."

"Ugh." I groan. Then, to Rebecca, I ask, "You haven't trained that out of him?"

She rubs his upper arm again. "Nope."

I quickly change the subject, so I don't have to see the smug look on his face. "So, did he tell you Jasper and I are gunning for his job?"

She laughs. "Something like that. It's so exciting! Are you still keeping the shop, though? It would be a shame for all those lovely antiques to go back into storage."

"Of course. As much as I hate hearing the cash register ding every time one of my precious babies walks out the door, I love seeing them all on display. It's how they were meant to be. Seen and admired."

"Truly," she replies. "It takes everything I have to not buy up all the items I see during my estate sales. It's a slippery slope. Once I let myself have one…"

"Well, now that I have an entire basement to fill up, you can be sure you're gonna see a lot more of me." For a moment, my smile drops, remembering everything that happened at her last estate sale. The women who made snide remarks behind my back, and the events that unfolded after I bought Mr. Foster's painting. But then I remember how nice Rebecca was and how she steered the women away from me, selling them the most expensive things in the whole house. And my smile returns.

Em taps me on the forearm. "Do not fill that basement up with stuff. It's perfect as it is."

It warms my heart that she's so supportive of my new venture into detective work. At least *one* of my best friends is. But maybe now that Chase sees how excited Rebecca is about it, he'll come around.

"Oh, don't worry," I reply. "I have plans for all the extra furniture."

Everyone exchanges reticent glances around the table, then all eyes land on me, waiting.

"You just bought an entire house. You need furniture." I say it like it's the most obvious thing.

"Is this just a ploy to make room for more stuff you bought that I don't know about yet?"

"No, but-"

"Actually," Rebecca says. "I have another sale coming up next weekend…if you're gonna have room."

"Oh dear," Em and Chase say at the same time.

I'm about to make some witty comeback when Waldo arrives with our food. He sets down Em's salad and Jasper's fettuccini Alfredo, and my chicken tenders. Then, the stench of herring assaults the entire table as he sets down *two* plates of it in front of Chase and Rebecca.

"You have got to be kidding."

Rebecca shrugs. "I love herring."

Chase's smug expression was unbearable. He's been waiting for this.

I don't give him the satisfaction of reacting. Instead, I dig into my tenders with gusto.

About halfway through, I feel a calm stillness settle over me. And I realize now that Em has Eddie and Jasper has Maura—as much as I still don't like that—I'm the only single one. Our entire friend group dynamic has changed so much lately.

But I'm fine with that, too. Maybe now that they'll all be busy with their own lives, they'll stop pestering me to date.

And stop worrying so much when I go chasing murderers around town.

Chapter Two

GUMSHOE WITH GUMPTION

FANZELA, C. (LAN) - Well, dear readers, Landrum's own antique dealing amateur sleuth is at it again. Many of you may remember the glowing reports we've presented to you of late about one Ms. Juniper Caine. Since returning to Landrum less than a year ago, Ms. Caine has been quite busy opening her antique shop, Juniper's Jewels, downtown and solving a slew of murders in her spare time.

Most of us never come across one unsolvable mystery or major crime. Yet, somehow, Ms. Caine has fallen head first into three within just as many months. First, she stumbled upon a decades old bank heist conspiracy that lead to the death of the man we all knew and some of us loved as Norman Foster. Then, as if that wasn't enough, Ms. Cain was quickly embroiled in the bad blood surrounding Ms. Evelyn St. James and her wayward daughter, Olivia Sullivan. Then, against all odds, Ms. Caine found herself caught up in some rather juicy—thankfully out of state this time—family drama involving adultery, sabotage, and good old-fashioned jealous rage.

Now, I'm not one to point fingers, especially not at one of our dearest and possibly most famous residents. However, at what point do we wonder how, or more accurately why, an innocent antique shop owner keeps finding herself caught up in so many illegal activities? Do we owe it to ourselves and our safe little beloved town to ask the hard questions?

September 2, 2023

Saturday

I'm so excited. The day is finally here. I've been looking forward to this estate sale ever since Rebecca told me about it, especially after tagging all the things in my shop I'm sending to Em's soon. So much space to fill with so many new things.

As I approach the unassuming red brick house, I'm struck because I never knew it was here. Greenwood Road isn't too far out of town, but I don't think I've ever been here. I also can't place the family name Adair. I don't remember going to school with any Adairs, or hearing any town gossip...an issue I plan to remedy with Ms. Minnie as soon as I relieve her of cat sitting duties.

Fluff was not happy about having adult supervision, but I've been letting them roam free too much lately. I got a call just last week from Mr. Robinson at the hardware store, telling me they were way over there. No, they might not like it, but it's for the best.

There are already a few cars lined up, and I don't want to park on the poor family's grass, so I leave my car out on the street and walk up. The closer I get, the more eerie the atmosphere.

It is an estate sale; I tell myself, though I don't think that's all of it. I'm getting a strange sense of déjà vu. If this house were a mansion like Mr. Foster's, I'd probably head back down the driveway and run. Maybe it's the quaint little garden and row of bright yellow flowered bushes lining the driveway that keep my feet moving in what I hope isn't the wrong direction.

Then, I see him and the déjà vu turns to dread.

Chase.

"What are you doing here? Did someone die again?" As soon as the words leave my mouth, they're followed by, "Just my luck," which I had no control over. Immediately, I'm hit with a gut punch of guilt. Someone *had* to die for there to be an estate sale. I let the guilt wash over me and dissipate. As harsh as it may sound, it kind of *is* just my luck for potential antiques for my shop to come with a dead body attached. It happened the last time I was at one of Rebecca's estate sales.

Rebecca. Of course.

Chase rubs the back of his neck, looking sheepish, and only then do I realize he's not in uniform. My body relaxes and my legs move more freely toward him and the house.

"Just keeping an eye on things." The way he says 'things' makes me wonder if he means Rebecca, or if there really is something to worry about with this family.

How in the world do I not know them? Once again, I remind myself to check in with Ms. Minnie about them. She's gonna love that. As one of the oldest townsfolk, she's also the richest source of everyone's business around here.

Still, I stop in front of him, hesitant to move forward. "Anything I should know?"

He goes to shake his head, then stops. "I think you'll love the prices." His grin is catlike and I get the impression he's trying to help his girlfriend have a profitable day.

Girlfriend. Might take some time to get used to that. But the way he beams with pride just by being here, I know she's good for him.

"Well then, I better get in there and snatch it all up."

I walk off and he calls from behind me, "I'll have Grady bring his pickup. He's off today."

Wow, Chase and Grady are both off at the same time? Must be a slow day for crime in Landrum. Yet again, as soon as the thought flies through my head, I hope I haven't just jinxed myself…and them.

The house is adorable. I'm a sucker for red brick. There's something so homey about them. Most of the houses around here are wood, sprawling two-story buildings with wraparound porches. Beautiful in their own right, yet this smaller square house steals my heart.

The front porch doesn't wrap around the house, and it's only two steps up from the ground, but it's got a lovely white column and plants galore. I'm noticing a theme. Too bad I run an antique shop or I'd buy a few of them. Maybe I will anyway. Butter Ms. Minnie up with new flowers for her store, not that she needs a bribe to spill the town's tea.

The door is wide open, so I let myself in. I don't think there are as many people here as there were at Mr. Foster's estate sale, though they're packed in a bit more tightly. I have to weave around a few old ladies to get to the sign in clipboard. I recognize some faces from my childhood, though most of their names escape me right now.

Most of the furniture is covered in white sheets, bringing back memories of old ghost movies, and that someone died. I wish I was wearing a jacket so I could tug it closed. So many things about today make me think of Mr. Foster and, investigation agency or not, I hope nothing like that happened to this nice family.

I shake my head and walk farther in, letting the coziness of the rest of the house comfort me. What furniture I can see is lovely. It's so lived in and inviting, a sharp contrast to the museum-like feel of Mr. Foster's house. I let that thought take hold and move farther yet into the living room.

And immediately regret it.

To my left is a closed door with yellow tape stuck to it, sealing it off from the rest of the house. Did Chase lie to me? Was there a murder in this house that he's trying to keep me from investigating?

An icy hand grabs my shoulder, and I jump.

"Sorry," Rebecca says in her sweet, soothing voice. Her perkiness from our lunch the other day is gone, replaced by her professional estate planner tone. She lets go of my shoulder and rubs her hands together. "Cold hands, warm heart, right?"

I give her a quick side hug, but I can't take my eyes off the door.

"Oh, don't get your detective brain started. That's just a safety precaution. This house isn't as structurally sound as it used to be." She sounds truthful enough, though I still look over her shoulder at the other customers. Nobody else seems to mind the strange sight, so I decide not to either.

"Where's the good stuff?" I ask, rubbing my hands together in anticipation.

"All of it's good," she answers with a very sales-y tone. "But I may have saved something special for you in there." She points to a door directly across from us. Though I've never been in this house, the placement of it feels like a dining room.

I'm confused as to why a dining room would have a door, and that hesitation causes Rebecca to give me a little nudge. I allow myself to be ushered forward, but pause for a deep breath before turning the knob.

If my past cases have taught me anything, it's that antiques come with more baggage than one might expect. So now I expect it.

The door opens into a long, narrow room with dark cream walls and even darker wood floors. The furniture, definitely not of the dining variety, is tucked away along the back wall and partially covered with the same white sheets. Some have been disturbed, as if other patrons hadn't respected the white sheets' warnings.

In the middle of the room, under brilliant golden white chandelier light, is my new—old, very old — roll top desk. Yes, Rebecca knew what she was doing when she set this baby aside for me.

I take a step closer and trace my finger along the rounded edges. This thing has seen many decades, probably a century or two. The teak wood finish is magnificently grained in a swirling pattern that runs the whole length of the tabletop. The hutch has a long, cylindrical version of an Edison light position just over the center of the desk. It's also full of small, cubby-like shelves that the previous owner had labeled with innocuous things like 'addresses' and 'maps' and 'correspondence.' It feels too intimate and personal to be out in the open. So I gently pull the two knobs on either side and roll the cover down to close the desk. It moves effortlessly on its track and lands with a soft click onto the locking mechanism.

I'm in love.

I don't want to leave it unattended in case someone else comes to claim it, but I must tell Rebecca I-

"I saved it for you," she says, as if she's been watching me the whole time and can see the dilemma on my face. "Go on, look around. It'll be here when you're ready."

"You," I say, putting an arm on her shoulder, "are an amazing salesperson."

"Yes, I am."

The rest of the house is full of the usual vestiges of life. More furniture than should fit in the square footage, even more trinkets and knick-knacks. I walk the length of the building twice, picking things up and putting them down. As I'm about to make my third trip around, it finally dawns on me what I'm doing.

Everything I consider buying, I first imagine how and why it could be a murder weapon. The ornately engraved letter opener? No way. The bronze statue of the woman and child with the super heavy base? Nope.

I look over at the other people milling about, carrying sharp and blunt objects out the door without a care in the world.

What are the odds?

I shake my head slowly. If Em was here, she would say I just jinxed myself.

With another quick shake, I grab the two nearest things—a pencil holder shaped like a book, and a tiny violin statue—and go find Rebecca.

After paying and telling Rebecca I'll be back with the moving truck in a few days for the desk, I send a bunch of pictures to Em and Lys.

My sister responds immediately with, 'Better not be haunted!'

Chapter Three

Sunday

Sir Fluffington III

"Please, can we stop?" Sassafras whines between labored breaths.

Sir Fluffington III is trotting a few paces ahead, with Spot holding rank between them. "We're almost there. I can see the door." He tries to make his tone sound authoritative, but he's feeling the burn in his hips and can't wait to lie down on the soft red couch.

Ms. Minnie stands at the door, waiting, but they're all moving so slowly. "You're late," she admonishes.

When she'd let them out earlier, she'd expressly said they had ten minutes. Not that anyone would expect three cats to understand such a thing, but they do. At least, he does.

But ten minutes isn't long enough for a good 'light jog' as Sir Fluffington III had lied to get Spot and Sassafras out the door.

As they limped past Ms. Minnie and into the cool air of the antique shop, it took all his willpower not to purr. No self-respecting cat of his age and stature would dare.

Ms. Minnie gave each one of them a treat, then wagged a finger at him specifically. "I have to get back to my flowers. I expect you to behave yourselves."

Before the door fully closes, Spot and Sassafras have scarfed up their treats and hopped up onto the couch.

"I think not," he says in his commanding tone.

They scooch out of the way. Sassafras even climbs onto the back of the couch, something Sir Fluffington III knows Miss Junie wouldn't like, but he's too exhausted to say anything. He settles into the middle of the couch and closes his eyes.

"Where's all the stuff?" Spot asks.

When Sir Fluffington III forces his eyes open, Spot is standing on his hind legs, looking over the back of the couch. He noses Sassafras, who reluctantly jumps down.

"Oh, wow." She, too, sounds confused.

Sir Fluffington III rubs his eyes on the couch to wipe the tiredness away, then goes to investigate.

As soon as he makes it around the couch, he's immediately disappointed in himself.

How did I not notice this?

There are several large empty spaces on the floor where furniture used to be and a lot of Miss Junie's things are missing. The long chest of drawers he used to stand on to meow orders is one of them. The tall lamp he liked to sharpen his claws on when Miss Junie wasn't looking was gone. The end table with the broken handle—his favorite hiding spot for napping—is gone. The fresh paint on the walls is visible again because the paintings are missing.

"You don't think..." Spot asks, apparently remembering last time a painting went missing from their shop.

He's about to respond when Sassafras pipes up instead. "This is what we get for exercising."

Spot makes a noise. "I barely broke a sweat."

They both look at him and he dips his head. "I said barely."

"It can't be..." Sir Fluffington III closes his eyes raises his nose in the air. It helps him think. He retraces their steps that morning, but they never went into the shop. When Miss Junie left, she had said something to Ms. Minnie, but he hadn't been paying attention. He was in too much of a hurry to get outside and exercise.

Alright, he admits to himself. He was in a hurry because he'd heard that Mariel was back in town.

When they'd started meowing to go out, Ms. Minnie opened the back door, and they ran. So now, with her and Miss Junie both gone, it's up to them to find out what happened.

Sassafras walks to the front door, sniffing. That kid's got a nose on her. After a moment, she looks back at them. "There's too many. I can't get a-"

Before she can finish the thought, there's a loud noise. The three of them all look in different directions. The sound echoed too fast for them to catch its origin.

He's about to tell them to stand firm, but Sassafras breaks and scurries under the long blue couch. Spot hesitates, and Sir Fluffington III can see him at war with himself. He wants to stay and fight, but his instinct is telling him to hide. When the bang reverberates through the house once more, Spot loses his resolve.

They both run toward the couch.

Sir Fluffington III tells himself he's just going under there to protect his subordinates.

When the noise happens again, it stops him mid-crouch. He gets ahold of his senses and looks over his shoulder to where he thinks the sound is coming from.

"I'm going to investigate."

Emerald

"No, farther against the wall." I point toward the kitchen, then motion for them to scoot to the left. "More."

Jasper groans, but I can't tell if it's at me for not being able to make up my mind, or Junie for giving me such a heavy dresser.

Chase, who's dragging the other end of the thing flush with the corner, says, "At least I don't have to go to the gym today. Austin's been hogging the rower. It's like he knows when I'm trying to work out and he only goes there to torture me."

Junie shoots him a look I can read so well. She won't say it, not in front of Jasper. She's been really good at holding her tongue lately. I'm so proud of her. But we can all read her face well enough to know she's thinking some version of, "Now you know how I've felt my whole life."

Jasper and Maura have been dating for months, but poor Junie only found out a couple of weeks ago. The wounds are still raw.

Although, I think it's pretty funny that Chase, of all people, now has his own mortal enemy. He was always the 'let's all just get along' type in school. Guess he's getting cranky in his old age...which is something *I* won't say out loud, either. Especially considering we all just turned thirty together this year.

Junie goes back to the moving truck with the boys to bark more orders, and probably to keep an eye on her fancy old furniture that's now my fancy old furniture. Either way, we're all running like a well-oiled machine.

When they return with the biggest piece, a beautiful dark wood desk that looks heavier than my whole new house, I almost feel bad telling them it goes all the way to the room in the back.

Jasper huffs as they pass me.

"Don't worry, you're gonna get a pizza after we're done."

Chase says, "A pizza EACH," with a loud grunt.

I shrug. As a favor to Jasper, I won't make him share a pizza with Chase, who loves anchovies as much as he loves herring.

Two hours later, when the truck is empty and everything is close enough to where I want it, we release the boys to go do the second half of their job today. Despite his exhaustion, Chase lights up, no doubt because he's going to see Rebecca. Then I catch him sniffing his armpit and glance at Junie to see if she also clocked it. One corner of her lip goes up in response.

"Would you boys like to freshen up first?" I ask, sweetly.

Chase starts to head toward my pristine new guest bathroom and I strong arm him. "There's a gas station on the corner."

Jasper uses the distraction to muscle past us and slam the bathroom door. Chase shrugs and gives me a smirk.

"Fine, but if you track one speck of grime in there, you're cleaning it up."

"Take it off the pizza fund." He grabs my hand that's still braced against his chest and wipes his nasty forehead with it.

I snatch my hand away and wipe it down his shirt, which does no good because it's just as drenched. "Ew, does Rebecca know you're this disgusting?"

"She finds it charming." He puts his nose into the air and walks down the hallway to wait at the bathroom door.

Junie and I both call after him, "For now!"

A few minutes later, when they finally leave, Junie and I start organizing the larger items that aren't in boxes. I'm carrying one of her enormous donated paintings into the back room with the desk when my phone buzzes. It's Eddie. 'Hey just got off. Still need help?'

I can't stop the smile that spreads across my face. Half at his sweet offer and half at his impeccable timing. I wonder if Chase texted him that the coast was clear.

'Always'

"Oh dear," Junie says as she comes up beside me with the matching painting to the one I just sat down.

"What?" I feign innocence.

She rolls her eyes. "I haven't seen that look on your face since Jimmy Rosen asked you to prom."

My cheeks burn, but I snap back. "Jimmy's got nothing on Eddie."

She makes a gagging motion and takes off.

"That's what you get for eavesdropping!"

"Where do you want these?"

I enter the room to see her attempting to hold up the large painting against the wall to my right. "I don't know. You think they'd look better together or across from each other?" I turn to the wall opposite and hold up my painting. "Wait, a minute…" I sit the heavy wooden frame on the floor, then look between the two. "Are these the ones you got from Rusty?"

Junie stares at her shoes, not speaking.

"Oh, no no no. You're not sticking me with your murder paintings!" I instinctively flip mine around to face the wall.

"They had nothing to do with the murder. They're just pretty. And they don't match the new office decor." From the way she's scratching her nose as she says it, we both know she's lying.

"Nothing to do with the murder besides you buying them directly from a murderer, then him hand delivering them to you in a definite attempt to intimidate or murder you!" I point at her painting and she turns it around to face the wall. Then I stalk back out to the living room.

She follows but stays behind me. When she speaks again, her voice is lower, more contrite. "I can't keep them. The cats just stand in front of them meowing. They don't like them."

"Oh great! They're totally haunted!"

"Stop! You're as bad as Lys."

"She thinks they're haunted, too?"

"No, but she thinks my new roll-top desk is."

"Well, with your luck."

She looks like she wants to say something more, but she goes to a pile of kitchen items and starts arranging them on the counter.

I decide to give her a break and change the subject. "Harry approved my new schedule. As long as I plan my trips far enough in advance, I have full control of my calendar. And I can train Roxy to take over some of the smaller stories."

"Oh, so you'll be around more? Finally! I've missed you."

"I've missed you, too. And yes. I'll be around. Jasper-" I catch myself. I don't want to admit that we talked about her and how my staying close was more of a babysitting job than a need to stay closer to home base for work.

Her gaze cuts across the entire house and bores down on me. She knows full well what it means.

She shrugs and smiles. "Can't wait! Maybe someone got murdered with my new desk after all and we can go on an adventure together!"

I smile back, but I'm not sure I'm ready for all that. Her adventures have been getting out of hand lately.

Chapter Four

September 12, 2023

Tuesday

Juniper

'The cats have been acting so weird today' I text Em.

'As apposed to...when they act normal?'

'Hey!' I reply with only my thumb.

The phone is on my lap hidden under the counter while I watch the tall, large man peruse my typewriter section. The baby blanket I've been making for the hospital for way too long is also in my lap.

While I'm at it, I text Charlotte at the Ladies Council of Landrum that the blanket is almost done. Her reply is a gif of someone laughing hysterically followed by, 'better late than never!' Hopefully, that's enough motivation to get me over the finish line. I'm so close, if I can just focus.

The big guy is not my usual customer, especially not for typewriter sales. My senses are all on edge, watching him, waiting for something to happen. This time, I'm ready. After the Rusty incident—which is probably why this big guy has me all worked up—Chase made me install a panic button. As long as I stay right here beside it, my blood pressure is still within the normal range.

The cats are acting weird, though. Fluff won't leave my side. Spot's stalking the customer like a security guard, and Sass...well, Sass is napping. Even so, two out of three is bad.

'Are they movers there yet?'

'No, but soon,'

I take a deep breath. That's right. The movers are on their way. Chase got called back to the station when he and Jasper were on the way to pick up my desk and I had to make other arrangements. Good thing I still had a little left over from Ms. Evelyn's retainer. It's gone now, but I'm proud of myself for putting it to good use.

So yeah, everything's fine. The movers will be here soon. If big guy over there tries something I'll have-

"Ma'am?"

I hadn't realized I'd closed my eyes until I open them to find the big guy standing right in front of me. Had I lost track of him? How long were my eyes closed? Or is he just that fast?

All these thoughts run through my head as I plaster on my customer service smile. "Yes, how can I help you?"

He points over his shoulder at the row of typewriters. "Can you give me some advice? I can't decide." Without waiting for my response, he turns and walks back to the typewriters, all the way across the room, far away from my panic button.

Fluff and Spot are right on his tail, and I steel myself to come out from behind the counter. I don't know if seeing their bravery gives me a bit of encouragement, or if I'm worried they'll jump on him because they're so tense. Maybe both.

I set the baby blanket on the counter next to a beautiful new dish set I just got from a yard sale. As with everything else in here, I haven't been able to make myself put a price tag on it yet. Of course, my rationalization is that I need to do my research. I saw an old book on antique pottery and fine dining sets in Mr. G's shop. I could go tomorrow and-

I feel the big guy's eyes on me and realize I haven't moved an inch. "Sorry, I was…" I held up the blanket. "Marking my spot."

"Oh, congrat…" He quickly glances at my abdomen then back up, unsure how to finish that sentence.

"No, it's for the hospital. Population's booming in Landrum. Gotta keep those babies warm!" I have no idea what the population of Landrum's doing, but it's better than us focusing on my midriff. I think I'm still full from all that pizza the other day.

"That's very kind of you. I was actually a preemie, so I really needed extra blankets."

I look up, way up, at him and I'm sure my mouth is hanging open.

"Yeah, hard to tell now, huh? Must have been all those blankets." He gives me a kind shrug. Then he nods toward the first typewriter. "It's between this one and that one over there." He points to one at the end of the shelf.

My heart sinks.

These are two of my favorites and I don't want to lose either. Why did I think opening an antique store was a good idea?

I lovingly caress the late 19th century Blick #7 and try to cover the sorrow in my voice. "As you can see, this one is more of a bare bones style with an exposed carriage, and its own oak case, which I never close because why would you? It's functional, but parts are very hard to come by now, so use at your own risk."

I force myself not to frown as I make my way to the end of the row. "This Underwood #5 is more 'modern' if you want to call it that, with the curved type bar. While still relatively open, the frame is sturdier and more ergonomic. Again, parts are hard to find, but this one is also functional."

I chew on my lip to keep my face steady.

He studies me for a moment. "Is this difficult for you?"

"A little," I admit. "I've had them both for a long time."

"Well," he says, backing up and making a show of perusing the whole row again. "Is there any typewriter here that you could sell me without it breaking your heart?"

I don't bother to look. "Probably not, but I got myself into this mess." We both laugh and I feel some of the tension leave my shoulders.

"Alright then, I'm going to take that one." He points at the Blick. I nod and move to grab it to take it to the counter. "No, here let me." He gently closes the case and holds it out between us. "Would you like to give it one last pet before I go?"

Yes, I would, but I shake my head. It's better this way. Rip the Band-Aid off.

We walk to the sales counter and I ring him up. It's a decent commission, which I know I need, but it still stings.

As I hand his card back, he says, "I'm sorry. But if it's any consolation, you're going to make my grandmother a thrilled woman. Her birthday is next week, and she's going to love this."

Awww. Almost makes up for it.

He picks up the typewriter and moves toward the door but stops. "You know, if you're not doing anything-"

A muffled banging sound interrupts him and we both stand there, frozen. When the bang happens again, he closes his mouth and frowns, then leaves with my favorite typewriter.

I follow the noise toward the living room and the cats—Sass included—run in front of me. My phone buzzes, but I've left it all the way over on the counter. I'm about to go back for it when I hear the banging again and realize it's knocking.

I run down the basement stairs in the living room floor and hurry to let the movers in.

"I'm so sorry. I didn't hear you."

There are two of them, one huge and older, and one younger, with the same face minus some lines. They're both holding one end of my new antique roll-top desk. The larger one in front grunts, but forces a smile as sweat runs down his temple. "All good, ma'am. Where do you want it?"

I motion for them to just set it right inside the door. I don't have the heart to make them carry it any longer.

After I pay and give them a healthy tip for their troubles, I text Jasper and send him a picture of the desk by the wall.

'Gonna need your big strong muscles,'

'Out with "You Know Who," but I'll be there tomorrow'

My face contorts in disgust before I rein it in. I really need to work on my feelings toward Maura.

'Fine. We need to figure out a better doorbell system while we're at it.'

Sir Fluffington III

Sir Fluffington III stands atop the stairwell, looking down at Miss Junie and the two strange men. "Spot, on duty."

"Yes, sir." Spot runs down the stairs and meows in his deepest voice at the two men.

Before he can give further orders, Sassafras runs halfway down to sneak a peak. "They're carrying a really big table. It looks so scratchable."

Curiosity gets the better of him and he meets Sassafras on her middle step. His claws stretch out, but he reels them in. "I'd advise against it, little one."

Her ears flick. He forgets she's not that little anymore and part of him misses the little ball of furry energy that would chase him and Spot every time they stepped outside.

She sniffs the air. "They don't smell like the noise."

Sir Fluffington III disguises his laugh as a sneeze. He's going to miss her funny little sayings when she's fully grown. It reminds him of how Spot used to call food 'nummies,' though he'd never admit it now. "No, you're right. It doesn't smell like whatever's been making that noise."

The noise in question has been haunting them for days. Every time he thinks he's close to catching the culprit, it stops. His first suspect was the little beast living in the kitchen, but in all his years on the streets, he'd never heard a mouse make such a sound. Not to mention the fact that it never comes from the same place, or really from one place in particular. It's like something is all around them, scratching and rumbling different parts of the house just to mess with him.

So far, it doesn't seem like Miss Junie or any of the other humans who come in and out of here have noticed it.

"Do you think it sounded like them?" Sassafras noses toward the two men who are leaving.

Spot looks back at him for instructions and he nods for them to follow him up the stairs. "No, at first I did, but the noise is bigger. It moves around the whole house. Besides, we've heard knocking before. We'd know if that was it."

"Yeah, I suppose you're right."

"But we're gonna keep our ears up, regardless."

When they reach the top of the stairs, Sir Fluffington III realizes they have the perfect opportunity for some investigating. Now that Miss Junie has her pretty new table, she won't be paying much attention to them. "Spot, go check out those dishes again. Make sure you notice nothing out of the ordinary."

"Starting to forget what that looks like around here, sir," Spot says as he marches off, tail and ears up.

"You," he says to Sassafras, "stay close to the stairs just in case. I don't expect too much trouble right now, considering she's down there by herself. But like Spot said, we just can't be sure these days."

He sees Sassafras stretch and her nose twitches a little too happily.

"No scratching."

Her shoulders slump. "I wasn't gonna."

He doesn't bother arguing with her as she slinks off. This will be a good opportunity for her to practice her stalking while she's at it.

For his assignment, he posts up on top of the highest shelf beside the beaded curtain door. He nudges over a figurine that looks like an eagle with a rose in its beak. Garrish if you ask him, but nobody is.

He sits tall with one eye on Sassafras at the stairs and the other on Spot by the sales counter. From this vantage point, he can watch both his charges in case they get into trouble. He can also take a moment to think.

With two new items in the shop, he has to be ready for anything. It's unclear how a table or a set of dishes could be involved in a murder, but he's sure they're about to find out.

He starts mentally planning his course of action should either or both become an issue. He'd send Spot out to chase down leads and let Sassafras sneak around listening to conversations. And he'd stick to Miss Junie's side like gravy on chicken.

His stomach rumbles. Then it happens again and he realizes it's not him. It's the noise.

In a flash, all three of them are chasing it...in three different directions.

Chapter Five

JUNIPER

I switch the phone camera to selfie mode and position myself away from the desk as I wait for Lys's face to pop up. When it does, it's covered in flour and glitter.

"Um," I say, confused.

"Biscuits and butterflies," she says, as if that helps.

"Should I call back?" I raise my finger to hang up the call.

"No, it's fine. Not like we're gonna get any *less* messy later. What's up?"

"I just wanted to show off the office. It's almost organized just how I want it."

Lys mouths something to one of the kids off screen and even though it's silent, I hear the mom voice anyway. Then she looks back and says, "Oh, did the desk arrive?"

"Yeah, just a few minutes ago. I was upstairs and—oh, you won't believe the horrible news."

"What?" She says it so fast and full of worry, I immediately feel guilty.

"No, nothing like that. Sorry. I sold the Blick." I frown pitifully, but Lys's face is blank. "The super old gorgeous one-of-a-kind typewriter."

"Oh, I bet you got a pretty penny for it then." Leave it to my big sister to see the silver (or gold) lining in me losing my precious belongings.

"Yeah, I did alright. I was actually just ringing the guy out when the movers-"

Her tone perks up. "Guy?"

"Customer."

"Guy customer who likes super old typewriters...What did he look like? Give me the deets."

I groan. "Nobody says deets anymore, Lys."

"Quit stalling."

"There are no *deets*. He was buying it for his grandmother's birthday." I definitely don't add that I think he was about to ask me to go with him when the movers interrupted. Or that I was actually going to consider it, if only to make sure my beloved Blick went to a good home.

"Awww," Lys says, interrupting my mini daydream. "Tell me he was cute."

"He was way too huge to be cute," is the last thing I should have said.

"Juniper! Please tell me you got his number!'

"Can you please stop trying to fix me up and look?" I flip the phone camera to show her the desk.

"Why is it against the wall?"

"Jasper's coming to move it tomorrow. Gives me time to clean it."

"It's gorgeous. Just your type," Lys says, and I can't help but chuckle. Yes, typewriters and desks are way more my type than any man she tries to shove in front of me.

I walk her around the room, showing off the fresh paint and filing cabinets. Then I move to the center of the room where my desk will soon be, right beside Jasper's antique but not nearly as awesome one. "I'm glad I changed my mind and didn't get the fancy new metal one I sent you the link to. This is definitely more my speed."

"It's adorable, yeah, but I hope your speed is slow."

I turn the phone back to face me so she can see my irritation. "I wish you would just be happy for me. I've found something I like doing and Jasper's here to keep me safe."

"Chill, I wasn't talking about that. I've almost given up on stopping you from chasing murderers around town. Almost. I was just saying it's going to be hard getting much work done on a roll top. Is there even room for a monitor?"

"We'll see. I think I can put one on the top and just angle it down. I'll send some pics when it's all set up."

"And what about the shop? How's that going...aside from you letting the man of your dreams waltz out the door with the typewriter of your dreams?"

"Check it out for yourself," I say, decidedly ignoring her joke. We walk upstairs to the shop and I show her around.

"Look at all the empty space. Great job!" She says that in her mom voice, too, and I don't have the heart to tell her it's empty because I *gave* it all away to Em.

"And look at this," I say, changing the subject. I point the camera at the stack of antique dishes. They're bright white porcelain with intricate blue lined filigree. Spot is sniffing around them and I shoo him away. Last thing I need right now is for him to break one. "It's a full set. Can you believe my luck?"

"Didn't Grandma Barrett have some just like that?"

"Similar, yeah. But I actually think these are older, and having the complete set is so rare."

"How much did you pay for that?"

"Not much, actually. The guy running the yard sale must not have known what..." I trail off, my mind running full speed. "Hey, what if he was just trying to get rid of them? What if these are my new case? I wonder how you kill someone with a porcelain bowl without breaking it?"

"Hardy har har. Don't even play about that."

"Don't you have some butterfly pancakes to make?"

"That's not..." She shakes her head. "Whatever happened with your last 'case?'" She even finger quotes the word case.

I shrug. "Last I heard, he was gonna plea to keep the whole affair business off record."

"Probably for the best. That was so scary."

I nod in agreement. Seeing the hulking frame of someone I thought was my friend coming after me like that. It was terrifying. Just goes to show you never really know someone.

Then, almost as an afterthought, Lys asks, "Was typewriter guy bigger than him?"

"A lot."

After hanging up with Lys, I head back downstairs to clean the desk. Rebecca did a great job, and it doesn't really need to be wiped down again, but I need an excuse to stare at it and touch it. Fluff follows me, so close I almost trip over him. I would not forgive either of us if I fell down the stairs and died before getting to sit at my new desk. I've always wanted a roll top and now I finally have one.

I go to the little supply closet I had the contractors build for me and grab a bottle of furniture wax and a cloth. I've used this square of my old night shirt for years and it feels natural in my hand. The smell alone is enough to pump me up for some good old-fashioned polishing.

Lys's words keep ringing in my head as I start. Typewriter guy was bigger than Rusty, and I walked around the shop alone with him. I didn't get a vibe or anything, though I don't think I got one from Rusty either. I try to think back to the time Mr. Davenport—as I remember him—came into the shop. The first time, I don't recall having any gut feelings.

I really need to work on my danger radar. Maybe there's some kind of class I can take along with the self-defense course Em signed us up for. That's her way of pitching in and supporting me on this journey. It's funny how she went from pushing me into this to begging me to back off. Learning how to kick some butt feels like a happy medium.

Plus, I still haven't started that licensing course Jasper signed me up for. I don't know what my hold up is. I hounded him for a week to get that set up and then...froze? At first, I told myself I was too busy with actual cases. Then the self defense class and gearing up for the family reunion. Who has time to become a legit Private Investigator?

The whole time my mind is whirring about my cases and messy life, my hands are busy polishing the desk up perfect. If I could only get this drawer back in. It came out fine a minute ago, but now that I'm done wiping it, the darn thing is stuck open. I set the rag and furniture polish down and sit on the floor in front of the drawer to get some leverage. The last thing I want is to push the thing off its track. If I thought getting typewriter parts was hard, I'm sure this would be near impossible.

Gently, I wiggle the drawer, placing one hand on each side to try to coax it back. Then I pull it farther out and push, but still nothing happens. It's like there's something blocking it. Maybe the track is bent, and I just didn't notice when I opened the drawer.

I use the tried-and-true method of checking the other side. I crawl across the floor and pull out the matching drawer. It glides out then in with no problem.

I lean back to my original position in front of my stuck drawer and think. The smart thing to do is probably wait for Jasper or someone else to come help. But I also know if Jasper breaks anything on my desk, I'll never forgive him. If anyone's gonna break it, it has to be me.

I take a moment to run my fingers along the sides of the drawer in a last ditch effort to fix it. Then I close my eyes and push.

The drawer shoves back into place with a loud thud. I'm so afraid that when I open my eyes, I'll see it hanging off the track sideways, but when I do, it looks perfect. The front panel is flush with the frame and perfectly straight. I let out my breath in slow relief.

Grabbing the wax and rag, I'm about to push myself up when I see what caused the loud thud. There's an old leather diary laying on the floor beneath the desk. It's a soft, worn brown book with dark straps wrapped around it. In the middle of the cover is an old metal key that looks like it should unlock a magical wardrobe to an enchanted land.

There's clear packing tape on either side. The tape is ripped and twisted and I know immediately that this is what I'd been pushing against.

I also know there's no way I'm touching it.

I pull out my phone and start snapping tons of pictures, which I send to Jasper and Em. Before they have time to go through, I'm calling.

It rings several times before going to voicemail. I hang up and try again. And again.

Finally, he gets the hint. "Junie," he whispers, "I told you I'm out-"

"Did you get 'em?"

"Get what?" He's still whispering, but I'm not. I can barely contain myself.

"The pics! I just sent them. Look and then get your butt over here!"

"I can't go over there. You know I'm on a date."

The word alone makes me sick. But this is more important. "I know. She can come, too."

I hang up before he can argue. Then I call Em.

"Did you get 'em?" I ask again.

"What is it? Where did you find that?"

"It was in the desk."

"Your new one?"

"Yes!"

There's a sharp intake of breath. "I'm on my way! I'll call Jasper."

"I already did. He'll be here in a few."

Em pauses and I know she's doing the math.

"Yes, I know he's bringing *her*. I can't worry about that now. We have a case!"

Emerald

I hang up the phone and look at Eddie. "I'm sorry, I have to go."

"Emergency at the ol' detective agency?" It's what he's begun calling Junie's shop, and it concerns me how right he is.

"Yeah, she found something strange and Jasper and I are gonna go check it out. Wanna come?"

"Absolutely not. I'm staying as far away from this as possible. Poor Chase." He gets up and pours his drink into the sink. "Want me to keep going?"

I frown. I'd forgotten we were in the middle of date night. He came over with a ton of food...well, ingredients for this amazing Greek dish I had on my last assignment. It was so good I couldn't stop talking about it so he decided we should try to recreate it. And now I'm about to leave him to run to Junie.

"I'm so sorry."

"No, don't be. You promised to be more involved, and I know how much you worry. I tell you what, leave this to me and I'll call you when it's almost done. If you're still out, we can decide what to do with it then. Maybe I can bring it to you. I've never taken a girlfriend dinner on the job before."

We both freeze.

We've been dating for months, and it's the worst kept secret in town, but neither of us has officially called each other...that...before.

I cough to mask a choke when I try to speak. Then I finally get out the words. "I've never had a boyfriend bring me food...ever."

His face lights up. "Then I'm definitely gonna be the first."

"Can't wait. You sure you're good here alone?" This is another 'never' for me. Not that I've had a house before, but I've never left any man alone in my place.

"Of course. I'll keep myself occupied. How about I get some of the old stuff out of that room and move it to-" He must catch a look on my face because he stops. "It's not going anywhere, is it?"

I shake my head slowly. "It's all from Junie."

"Obviously." He chuckles and stirs the pan of red potatoes. The smell is glorious and my stomach grumbles at me for planning to leave. "But do you mean *for* her, not from?"

"Same diff." I step out of the kitchen to stop torturing myself. It's gonna be at least two hours before I can eat any of it. I distract myself by putting on my boots and wrapping a shawl around my shoulders, although it's probably still eighty degrees outside. They match. What else am I supposed to do? "I know we won't be roomies now, but I still want Junie to have a nice work space here...just in case."

"In case her place is a crime scene one day?"

"Don't joke about that!" I give him a stern look as I open the door. But yes.

Chapter Six

JUNIPER

I don't know how long I've been standing here, staring at the diary.
I want to reach out and touch it so badly. The leather looks soft and
inviting, and there's a tiny placeholder string sticking out the bottom
that's just calling to me.

I squeeze my hands into fists and put them in my lap. I haven't
moved from the floor either. My back is killing me and the cats are
milling about, looking concerned. I don't think they've ever seen me
on the floor this long, and if I am, it's only to play with them.

I'm about to grab my phone and call Jasper again when I hear the
doorbell buzz upstairs. The cats and I all jump. Why wouldn't Jasper
use the new office doors I paid so much money to have installed?

"Well, don't just stand there, go let him in," I say to Fluff. He gives
me an unimpressed look and walks to the bottom of the stairs before
giving me an annoyed meow.

Spot and Sass run to him as if being called to attention.

"Fine, I'll get it." I push myself up and groan. I think something happens to you the night before you turn thirty that makes floor dwelling impossible.

When I make it to my feet, the cats look like they're whispering to each other.

"Wait till you're thirty!" I tell them with a huff before ascending the stairs.

There's another knock, this time more urgent. I quickly realize it's not Jasper. His knocks...when he bothers to knock before barging in...are faster and more hyped up like a woodpecker. These sound more like TV cops with a search warrant.

Am I being investigated?

I think back to the scathing article in the paper after the Rusty situation. That darn Fanzela and his determination to break a story that doesn't exist.

But no, if it was Chase, I'd recognize his knock, too. Wouldn't I? Maybe his work knock is different from his normal knock.

When I finally make it up the steps and look out the window, I see a tall, handsome man. He's not as big as typewriter guy, but I still have to crane my neck to meet his gaze as I get closer. He's got dark reddish brown hair which lightens as it turns into a beard and mustache.

I look at my phone screen for the time and realize I've been down in the office longer than I thought. "Hi, sorry about that," I say, unlocking the door. "Doing some renovations and...how can I help you?"

"Hi, thank you. I'm sorry to interrupt. I was just walking by and saw your sign." He points up above his head as he ducks through the doorway. "I'm looking for something nice for my mother, maybe a bracelet or a-" His hand goes to his neck before he looks around more closely at the shop and doesn't finish his sentence.

Juniper's Jewels strikes again.

"Ah, yes. I really need to reconsider that name. I'm Juniper." I stick out my hand and he takes it. "And these are my jewels." I wave my other hand at the assortment of antiques behind me. "Lucky for you, there is some actual jewelry among all the other things."

He lets go of my hand and walks farther into the shop. Normally, I've trained myself to stay by the counter, close to my panic button. But for some reason, I easily follow him deeper toward the back of the shop. If I was a more self-aware woman, I might call myself out for letting his handsomeness sway my decision. But I'm not. So I won't.

"Wow, I think this is even better. I didn't know something like this existed here in Landrum."

"It wasn't. I just opened. Are you from here?" I study his features, trying to recognize something, someone, from my childhood.

"I was. Left a long time ago but I'm back for a visit. How about you?" He smiles and flashes perfect white movie star teeth.

"Same...well, except I came to visit and didn't leave." I close my mouth hard to fight the powerful urge to slip in the fact that I came home after a breakup.

Get ahold of yourself, Juniper!

"Nice to come home sometimes." His bright blue eyes scan the shop and we both notice at the same time that all three cats are standing by the basement stairs, glaring at him. "Your security guards are on duty, I see."

"Yes, they're great. And so cheap! Couple cans of tuna and they're good to go."

"That's convenient. So, do you have any suggestions?" He motions to the half empty room.

"Yes, of course. Since you came here looking for jewelry, we can-"

"Actually, now that I'm here, I think mother would much prefer something with a bit more character." He puts a finger to his lip and turns slowly around.

"What does she like? I have furniture, art, lighting, figurines..."

"I...think...she'd like something more personal. Something lived in, you know? History."

"Well, you've come to the right place. I know the history of pretty much everything here." I don't add the fact that I know all this because it's *my* history. I pick up a set of tall candle holders that look like they came off the set of Phantom of the Opera. "These were donated by a company renovating an old Victorian house in Louisiana."

"Wow, road trip."

"I traveled a lot after college," I say. "How about a rare dinner service set?" I move toward the sales counter, where the dishes are still stacked. "These just came in recently. They remind me of some of my grandmother used to have and-"

"Oh, I couldn't." He stops and points me toward a back wall of lamps. "Mother has a lot of those."

"Ah, great choice." I follow him to the back of the store and the cats weave between our feet. "Stop it," I whisper, yell at them. "You're gonna trip someone."

They don't stop, but they stick closer to me. I guess if I fall, it's less of a problem than letting a customer fall.

The man scratches his beard and squints his eyes at the row of lamps. It's obvious none are speaking to him. "I don't know. I was thinking something more...personal. Something like-

There's a loud noise and I jump. The man grabs my arm to steady me and the cats hiss at him. He lets go.

"That didn't sound good," he says, his eyes running the length of the shop.

"I know. It's happened a few times lately, but I can never pinpoint where it's coming from." I put my hand over the spot on my arm where he'd held me.

I think it's gonna bruise.

Jasper

Jasper pulls the car into the side alley by Junie's shop and comes to a stop under the shade of a gigantic oak tree. He puts the car in park but doesn't move to get out.

"You ready?"

Maura's arms are folded against her chest and she's staring out the window at the building. "This is ridiculous, Jasper. Can't you see what she's doing?"

Jasper runs a hand through his hair. It's getting longer than he realized, longer than Maura likes. He makes a mental note to swing by the barber shop before their next date. Which, depending on how today goes, might be never.

He's taken too long to respond, so Maura keeps going. "There is no 'case.' It's just an old book. Junie's been obsessed with books her whole life. She doesn't need your help to figure out what that one is. It's just an excuse to ruin our date." Her arms squeeze tighter over her chest.

"She doesn't want to ruin our date. And you have to admit, it's kinda strange. A book stuck to the underside of a desk..." He can't help the pleading sound his voice makes. He wants this to go well so badly.

"The only strange thing I'll *admit* is her calling you—twice—when you already told her we were out. She knew what she was doing."

"I assure you, she meant nothing bad. She promised she would be nice." He doesn't dare add that Maura also promises the same thing.

"Nice. Yes." Maura plasters a vacant smile on her face and opens the door.

This is not gonna be good.

As Jasper's getting out of the driver's side, he sees a tall man walking out of the shop. A low noise escapes him before he can catch it.

"What?" Maura asks.

Jasper shrugs. "I don't know. I just got a bad feeling."

"Mmmhmm," she says with a scowl. "It's called 'jealousy.'

Chapter Seven

JUNIPER

"After you," I say to Fluff as he runs past me to go down the basement stairs first.

The handsome customer left without buying anything. I think that noise spooked him as much as it did me and the cats. Spot and Sass took off in opposite directions, trying to find the source. Fluff and I decided we were better suited for finishing up in the basement.

Besides, Jasper and Em should be-

The office door squeaks open and Jasper pokes his head in. I can see in his eyes that he's not having a good day. Then, when Maura appears behind him, tight-lipped and arms folded, I remember why.

I'd been so preoccupied with the handsome—making a sale—I forgot he was bringing her with him.

Happy thoughts, I remind myself. Where's Em? She's always been much better at schmoozing than me.

"Hey," I say, trying to fill my voice with sunshine and roses to match the smile I hope is showing on my face. "Just in time." I point toward the journal still waiting for me on the floor.

"Who was that?"

"Huh?"

"Who was that guy?"

"Oh, a customer. Well, he was gonna be a customer, but then that noise happened again and-" I point behind me toward the top of the stairs.

He makes a noise in his throat but doesn't say whatever else is on his mind. Then he steps farther inside, holding the door for Maura. She forces a small, polite smile to cross her thin lips, but doesn't move beyond the doorjamb.

As Jasper makes a move toward the journal, there's another commotion behind him. Em, with all her jangly keys, is unmistakable. She tries to slither past Maura, who's still blocking the entrance, but her arms are already open wide to hug me. So, instead, she barrels past Maura and the door closes with a loud whoosh behind her.

That reminds me, I need to install the air hydraulic thing on the door to make it stop doing that. It only happens when the trapdoor above the stairs is open, but that's turning out to be all the time.

"Junie! Please tell me you haven't opened it without me! This is so exciting!" Em seems completely oblivious to the glare Maura shot at her. But I wouldn't have my Em any other way. Negativity just bounces off her.

"I would never," I answer as we hug. Her hair smells like the conditioner from her dye, but when we pull away from each other, I can't tell any difference. Did she re-color it the same shade of blue? I don't think that's ever happened since she got her first bottle of Manic Panic in tenth grade.

Em claps her hands together. "This is so exciting! I don't think I've been here when the case first starts."

"We don't know for sure that it's a case." We both know I don't believe that, but I'd like to be on record as saying it.

"Of course," Em says with a conspiratorial wink.

Jasper reaches behind me to pick up the diary, and I slap his hand away.

"What was that for?" He jerks his hand away.

I go to his desk and grab the kitchen tongs, then give them to him, along with a pair of plastic gloves.

"Seriously?"

Em laughs.

Maura makes an annoyed noise.

I point to the wall behind him at our new poster with the checklist he made me agree to. SAFETY FIRST is written across the top in big bold letters.

Sir Fluffington III

"Troops! Assemble!"

Sir Fluffington III reluctantly moves away from his post beside Miss Junie and takes up a new one atop Mr. Jasper's desk. As of now, it's the highest workable point to give him a good vantage point over his subordinates and close enough to the action to jump in if anything should go wrong.

Sassafras kneads the thin carpet under the desk. She always does this when she's excited. "What do you think is happening? What's that thing on the floor? It smells yummy."

Spot stretches and sniffs the air. Sir Fluffington III can tell he's itching to run back. "Sass is right. It smells old and..." He stops himself before echoing the 'yummy.'

"Alright," Sir Fluffington III nods over Spot's shoulder. "You check out the stranger. Stay close to her. Get a read on her motives."

"Not good," Spot answers immediately.

"Yes, but that's surface level tension. Find out what's really going on. And most importantly, is she a threat?" He doesn't wait for a response and turns to face Sassafras. The child is still working the carpet. "I need you to put those young ears to good use. Listen closely to what's being said over there."

They both purse their lips and perk their ears.

Mr. Jasper has set the object on the floor, and Sir Fluffington III can see that it's a book. Living with Miss Junie, they wouldn't dare mistake it for anything else. Though, as he strains to hear what's being says, he thinks Miss Emerald calls it a 'diary.' He doesn't know the difference between a regular book and a diary book, but he plans to find out.

When Miss Junie puts on a pair of gloves that match Mr. Jasper's and opens the diary, Sir Fluffington III jumps down from the desk to get a better look. He doesn't like her touching it at all, especially since he hasn't had time to investigate it. When she reads the words aloud, a mix of numbers and names, he gets a bad feeling low in his gut.

He would recognize that tone anywhere. She's excited to have a new case. And she's going to put herself in harm's way because of it.

Chapter Eight

JUNIPER

I pull on the clear plastic gloves before taking the journal from Jasper. I can't stand the way they feel against my skin, but I'm used to it. Mr. G has a lot of books he won't dare let me touch without gloves. And it's always worth the discomfort.

Something tells me this will be worth it, too.

Em squeezes my arm. "I can't believe I'm actually here for this part!"

"We don't know anything yet," I say to calm her and myself.

There's a low, barking laugh from Maura's side of the room and I glance up in time to see a look pass between her and Jasper. Definitely an 'I told you so' moment for them.

Now I have more than just my initial excitement pushing me to hope this will be our next case. And when we solve it, knowing how much she'll hate it will make me even more proud.

"Open it!" Em shakes my arm that she still hasn't let go of.

The journal nearly slips out of my hand, but I recover quickly enough for it to land on the desk, where I meant for it to be, anyway.

"Sorry," she whispers.

"Are we ready?" I don't wait for a response before undoing the dark brown leather strap. It's not tied or fastened in any way other than being wrapped three times round the journal.

The scent of old paper and ink hits me immediately, way more pronounced than just holding the journal. It's one of my favorite things about books. And this one, being obviously handwritten over a long period of time based on the page coloring, is a unique combination. I can tell whoever had this journal took their time making precise entries. Precise...but strange.

I have to squint to see the thin, neat lettering. Partly because of the yellowed paper, and partly because of the low light in this corner. I reach for the switch in the back of the desk's hutch to turn on the light, but nothing happens. As I take out my phone to use as a flashlight, I make a mental note to get a new bulb and maybe a cool chandelier to hang over my desk. Although, I've already gone through all the money from Ms. Evelyn's case, so this one better actually pay.

"L. Hewitt, December 22, 1926, 13:57-17:04. M. Vincent, December 23, 1926, 07:41-11:13. A. Bauer, December 24, 1926, 04:33-09:17. N. Jansen, February 13, 1927, 08:22-09:18." I stop reading. "What in the world?"

Jasper pulls on my shoulder and I move out of his way. He then leans over the book and his lips move like he's reading the list to himself. I never imagined him as a mouth reader—but I probably should have. He flips a couple pages and reads on. I crane over his shoulder to see, though he's so much taller. I get the sense of Maura's beady shark eyes boring into my back, which only makes me scooch in closer. When he's finally done, he points at a line and holds the book up toward me. "This name, S. Stafford...it's here multiple times, then it just stops...right here."

He hands me the book and I scan the previous pages for the name. Indeed, it shows up many times, almost from the beginning. Then on this page, there's a tiny sketch outline of an octagon beside the entry. I turn a couple of pages, then a few more. The dates go all the way to the present time; the last one being just six months ago. But S. Stafford is never mentioned again.

"This...is...amazing!" The thrill of discovery courses through me.

"Creepy," Em says, reaching for the book, then snatching her hand away.

"You're entitled to your opinion." I would tease her about losing her edge and being no fun now that she's dating a cop, but I can see the gleam in her eyes. 'Creepy' and 'amazing' are synonyms for Miss Emerald Irons.

"Look at this," Jasper says, pointing to a new page. I'd almost forgotten he was here at all. But the memory of him reminds me of his companion, and I get that feeling in the pit of my stomach again. I really must learn to control that.

"What?" I ask, leaning in again.

"These are different." He runs his finger across a batch of pages in the middle of the journal that aren't set up as a ledger like the ones in the beginning. These each have a name at the top, then a bunch of squiggles and more tiny symbols.

This time, I'm the one who whispers, "Creepy."

I quickly search for S. Stafford, and find it on one of the first pages in the section. Then again and again. Whoever this person is, they were important to...who?

"That's shorthand."

I jump at the sound of Maura's voice. She's so close. How did I not hear her sneak up on me?

Jasper beams as if she's solved the mystery of the pyramids. "Really? You can read it?"

"No," she says, kind of slinking back into her hole a little. "But I recognize it. A friend of mine from school—Becky Levinson..." She glances quickly at me and Em.

Becky Levinson was the second most horrible person from my childhood. I'd spent a lot of mental energy blocking her from my mind since high school.

"...took a class in college when she was studying journalism. She used to write me these crazy notes and make me decipher them." A smile forms on her lips and I don't like the way it makes the pit in my stomach churn. She's not supposed to have good memories of the time she made my life a living — Em wraps an arm around me and I catch my fists clenching. I open my hands slowly, hoping the manicure she forced me to get last weekend didn't rip the thin plastic glove.

Then, I can't believe I'm saying this, but I ask, "Can you see if she'll-"

Maura's head is shaking vehemently before I even finish. "I'm not dragging her into...whatever this is."

"This..." I say, motioning to the journal—diary, yes, definitely a diary of some sort—but Jasper cuts off whatever I'm about to say. Honestly, it was probably nothing helpful, anyway.

"This is a mystery that I'd love to solve." His voice is so calm and patronizing. The Maura I know and hate would eat him alive for it. But this Maura visibly relaxes. Disgusting.

Sensing the frazzled state of my nerves, I turn to Em and address her only. "Did you learn shorthand when-"

There's a derisive snort behind my back. I close my eyes as Em places a hand on my upper arm. "No, sorry. But I'm sure Harry knows someone." Then she smiles wickedly. "I'll have to endure a very long 'Back in my day' speech, but for you, I'll manage."

"You're such a selfless person."

"No, I'm not. You're gonna pay for this."

Jasper closes the diary and sighs. "Alright, ladies, what do we think?"

I throw up my hands. "I think we've got ourselves a case!" I glare at Maura, daring her to disagree, but she only picks at her fingernails. They're long and pointy, like shark claws. I chuckle under my breath and feel more of the tension falling away.

Em's eyebrows furrow, probably because to her it looks like I just laughed about having a murder to solve. "Before we get carried away..." She pauses, knowing I would usually make a snide remark about *her* always being the one to get carried away first. But I'm still thinking about shark claws and trying not to laugh for real. "Let's take a step back and figure out what we actually have."

"A case," I whisper in a sing-song voice.

Jasper rubs his hand over his face. "Really, all we have is a journal-"

"Diary," Em and I say at the same time.

"Huh?"

I give Em a quick nod to go ahead. "It's clearly a diary. Someone took a lot of time to write in this thing over...*decades*."

"And how is that different from a journal?"

"Because it's more intimate. Have you ever taped a *journal* under a desk?"

"No, but I've never taped a...diary under one, either." He says 'diary' low, like it's against the law for a boy to even know that word. "Are you saying some little girl kept-"

"Ugh!" I can't help the sound coming out of my mouth.

"Ok, sorry. But still...whatever we call it. This is all we have to go on. We don't know what it means."

"Yet," I answer. "That's why it's a case."

Everyone slowly looks around the room at each other, including Maura, then all eyes settle on me.

Jasper is the first to speak. "We have a case."

My entire body is practically buzzing with anticipation. Jasper and Maura have huddled off in the corner to whisper. I wish I had bionic hearing, though I don't need it. The look on her face is worth two thousand words. And every one of them gives me a warm glow of satisfaction.

Em is on the other side of the room talking on her phone, no doubt to Eddie. I forgot they had a date tonight, and I ruined it. But she wanted to be more involved in cases. And now she is. I'm sure he gets called back to the station a lot, too. Chase is always-

Chase!

I promised I'd keep him more involved in the cases, too. And now that we're officially calling the diary one, I need to call him. But how? Do I call and say, 'hey, we found a mysterious diary with names and dates in it and, based on my track record, we're totally convinced it's a murder'?

Em hangs up and comes back over to me. "Eddie's on the way. Did you call Chase?"

"I was gonna...how did you explain it to Eddie? It sounds insane when you say it out loud, right?"

She shrugs. "Gotta get 'em used to the insane early, June."

Still, I chew on my lip. "He's out with Rebecca right now. I don't want to mess up their date." I whisper the last part with a quick head jerk behind me where Jasper and Maura seem to go at it. For some reason, I don't feel the slightest bit guilty about ruining that one.

"Do it."

"Fine." I act like she's forcing me against my will, but we both know I needed and wanted the push. One of us should have a strong backbone in this relationship.

'Hey, sorry, but I think we found something. You should come to the office. Bring Rebecca' I add the last part without thinking, but it makes sense. Even if she wasn't his girlfriend, she's the one who sold me the desk. Then I laugh.

"What?" Em asks.

"Chase is so worried about us constantly stumbling on murders. What are the odds that twice now, the murder objects came to me through his new girlfriend?"

Em's mouth opens, then splits into a wide grin. "I don't know, but I definitely dare you to ask him."

"Nope. I asked you first. If you need to phone a friend-"

She gives me a playful shove. "I'm going upstairs to wait for Eddie."

I furrow my brow and motion toward the new door.

Em leans in and whispers, "No way I'm interrupting *that*."

Maura's standing against the door, one hand on the knob, with that tight-lipped scowl she always has. I can't wait to see how many wrinkles she gets because of it. Jasper's voice is too low, but obviously pleading. And I can't wait to see how many wrinkles he gets because of *that*.

I take this opportunity to steal Jasper's chair and roll it over to the desk to get a better look at the diary, happy to finally have some privacy with it. Again, I have to use my phone as a flashlight, so I can't jot down any notes except in my head. So far, I have a running list of any recurring names, of which there are too many, and recurring symbols, which feel easier to manage.

There are the usuals; check marks and Xs. But I'm more interested in the peculiar ones, like the octagon and something that looks like a long U, and another squiggle that a kid would use to represent water. But what do they mean?

I try to put myself in a killer's shoes.

Naturally, the check and X would mean yes and no, right? But yes and no...what? And an octagon? Does that mean 'eight?' Eight what? Did the killer follow each person exactly eight times then...what? I have no idea what the long U would mean. That one will probably have to be answered by whoever solves the shorthand for us. But the water squiggle has to mean water, right?

"Junie?"

I jump and fling my arm back, hitting Jasper right in the chest. "Geez! Warn a girl first."

"I did." His face is calm, but his neck is red. I don't have to look at Maura to know what her face is doing. I can hear it in her short, angry breathing. He juts a thumb behind him at Maura. "We're gonna get out—go..."

"Cool," I say, rescuing him. "Have a fun rest of your date."

He offers a faint smile and his eyes land on the diary. I can tell leaving is the last thing he wants to do right now. But I was already nice to him, so I only manage a quick, "No way you're making me wait until you come back."

He sighs. "Wouldn't dream of it."

My phone screen lights up and I see Chase has texted me twice. I must have been so caught up in the mystery that I didn't notice.

'On our way', the top one says.

At that exact moment, Em and Eddie come bounding down the stairs. "I can't wait for you to see how creepy this thing is!"

I look back up at Jasper, then Maura, then Jasper again.

"We're good. You kids have fun."

I give Rebecca a hug first, then Chase, which he clearly notices.

"Your girlfriend here has some explaining to do," I tease.

They shoot quick, bashful smiles at each other at my use of that word.

Rebecca crosses her hands out in front of her like she's ready to be cuffed. "You got me."

Chase wraps an arm around her shoulders and pulls her to his side. "Before I go arresting my...girlfriend...why don't you tell me exactly what you found?"

"Alright," I say with a shrug, "but keep those cuffs handy."

Em and Eddie are already standing over the diary, and we all gather around to examine it closer. I hold up my phone for light but Eddie pats my hand and I lower it. He pulls a bright flashlight out of his pocket.

"Wow, that's so much better." Now, with my phone free, I open my camera and start recording. "Obviously, we haven't seen anything yet that points directly to a murder. But this diary is creepy-"

"Journal," Chase interrupts.

"OK, *Jasper*," I warn him. "We've already cleared up that point. This *diary* is creepy. We can't assume a bunch of names and dates in an old handbound leather book is uncreepy. Why else would they tape it under a desk?"

"It was what?" Chase asks.

"Exactly!" I say in answer. Then I point to the spot behind the stuck drawer. "It was taped under there. Now, I haven't been in the detective biz for long, but-"

Chase groans, and Eddie stifles a laugh with the help of Em's elbow in his rib.

"You don't go through that much trouble to hide something non-murdery."

I wait for Chase to agree. He nods and adds a knowing glance at Eddie over our heads.

"What?" I ask.

"Nothing."

"Not nothing!" I turn my phone camera in his direction. "Spill it."

"I'm not at liberty to-"

Em and I both gasp. My phone is trembling in my hand, making Chase's image shake, when I get a text from Jasper.

'Please don't do anything without me.'

I turn off the recording and reply with a quick, 'Too late' before shoving it in my pocket.

Chase slowly nudges me and Em out of his way. "Eddie, do you have gloves? Junie, get me a bag."

"No!" I mean it to come out forceful, but it's more of a whine. This is what I get for being honest with him about my cases.

Eddie picks up the tongs Jasper had been using. "I don't have any bags, though."

Chase takes out his phone and after a moment says, "Grady, bring an evidence kit to Junie's." Then, after a brief pause, adds, "Yes...*again*."

Chapter Nine

Thursday

"At least let me see." Jasper makes a move for my phone and I hold it in the air away from him. "Really?" He easily stands a foot taller than me, but he doesn't swipe it from my outstretched hand.

"They're almost here."

"Come on, you two," Em says, like she's the responsible one in our group suddenly. She pats the cushion of her adorable new blue suede sectional. Eddie's already sitting on the other side. I wait, expecting him to pat his cushion for Jasper, and get a chuckle out of that image.

Mom and dad are angry.

"Mom—Em's right." I saunter to her and plop down. Then I make a show of behaving myself by looking around the room. "I love what you've done with the place."

She knows I'm teasing Jasper, but I really do love it. The walls are freshly painted shades of blue and green that make the living room feel warm and inviting. The artwork has hints of both blues and greens but with enough red and yellow thrown in to pop. I've never been able to decorate my stuff, but I can tell when it's done right, and this is it.

"Veronica came by last weekend and helped with the..." She points behind her at the wall, but I forget to listen. I'm too busy shoving down the bite of jealousy that claws its way up every time she mentions Eddie's sister. I know she'll never take my place, but what if she takes my place? If they get married, she'll actually be Em's *sister*-in-law. Just like she always wanted with me. But that would mean I had to marry Jasper.

There's that familiar pit in my stomach again.

The little brother in question is settling into the beat up old chair across from us. Definitely not part of the modern ensemble. I glance at Eddie, who's trying not to notice. Men and their recliners.

I don't blame Jasper for being impatient. When he texted for us to wait till tomorrow, none of us knew that tomorrow would be two days away. But Chase, Eddie, and Grady all stayed well into the evening to bag up the diary and check the desk for any additional evidence. I was practically banned from my own office. I did, however, sneak a couple of close-up shots and more video before they left. I even convinced Grady to thumb through the back pages for me so I could complete my recording.

Then, when Jasper and I both decided it was best if he stayed away yesterday, we also came to two other realizations. One, we need to come up with some rules of evidence chain of custody. Two, if we're gonna work together, his girlfriend needs to check her attitude. His version of number two might sound a little different, but that's my takeaway.

Unofficially, number three is regret over calling Chase so soon. He blames Em for telling me to do it, but I'm sure that's just a sibling thing. Was it the right thing to do? Up in the air. Did it leave us huddled in Em's new house looking at an incomplete record of what's in the diary? We're missing a sizeable chunk of the middle.

Jasper says, "Hope it's enough to get us started," as if he's been thinking the same thing.

Eddie's eyebrow goes up. "Hope what's enough?" Then I realize he doesn't know why we're here. I question Em with my eyebrow.

She shushes me before saying, "When Chase and Rebecca get here, we have a few things to discuss."

Eddie glances my way and I make a big show of admiring Em's artwork again. "Like what? Antiques?" He says the last word more like a suggestion than a guess.

"I'm sure that will be part of it," she answers. "I'm dying to show Junie and Rebecca what I've done with the room."

"The room?" I ask.

"Yes! Wait till you see it! You're gonna love it."

Before I can respond, the doorbell rings. It's one of those gothic sounding deep gongs that would fit right in at an old cathedral church. But, somehow, it fits here too. It's so her.

When Chase and Rebecca enter, Eddie jumps up and catches Chase by the arm. "I think we're needed over there." He points to the kitchen.

"Wha-" Chase is dragged away and the rest of that thought dies on his tongue.

Em and I both shrug.

Rebecca hugs us and we let Em show off the—my, obvious-ly—room. Everything I gave her is in here, set up beautifully like an office away from the office. The two hundred-year-old desk is posi-tioned in the center of the room, with the natural light from the wall of large windows shining directly on it. There are several paintings lining the other walls, some of which I don't recall giving her. She must have gotten those on her own, but they match perfectly with the ambiance. And best of all, there are floor lamps in each corner, each with their own unique—but similar enough—carved bases. Her intention is obvious. I don't even have to notice the big grin on her face, along with the pleading look in her eyes. This is my space in her house.

"I love it," I say, giving her a giant hug. "It'll be perfect for when I want...need to get away from you know who."

Jasper makes an exaggeratedly hurt noise. "You know who is right here."

"My point exactly."

"Whatever, we're all here. Show me the phone!"

I try to go back toward the living room where we all have our seats picked out, but he's not having any of it. He reaches for my phone and we fumble with it before I snatch it away.

"Here!" I pull up the video and let it play in its entirety, then we scroll through the fifteen or so pictures I took while Chase was bagging it.

"There's so much missing," Jasper complains.

"Yeah, well, it was me against the three of them because somebody left me all alone." Em nudges my rib and I shut up.

Rebecca whispers something that sounds like 'wow' then adds, "Is this what it's like every time?"

At first, I think she's commenting on our bickering, but she's staring at the phone screen, mesmerized.

"Yeah," I say. "It's such a strange feeling, especially now. You're sure in your bones there's something going on, but you still have no idea what."

Jasper starts the video over. "What do you know so far? Where are your notes?"

I think he expects me to take out a notebook like his, so when I tug on the phone to open my notes app, he tries to pull it away. I yank it. "Right here." I swipe over to my notes. "From what I gathered so far, the dates start in the mid 1920s and go through this year. Some names are in there a lot, and some only have a couple entries, then stop. I noticed, too, that some have the same last name but different first initial, so family members, I guess. The ones who have the most entries, it seems, are the ones who get their own pages. One name I saw a lot was E. Hess. They're in there from almost the beginning and all the way to-"

"Now." Rebecca's voice startles all of us.

"Um, yeah." I flick back to the pictures. "Here, on the last page. Why?"

When I look at Rebecca, her lips are sucked in like she's trying to keep herself from speaking. "I don't know if I'm allowed..."

Jasper steps toward her. "Beck," he says, as if they've been friends forever. Em and I both make ick faces. Oblivious, he keeps talking. "You're one of us now. You're in this. Junie got the desk from your estate sale. And...remember...she got the painting from your other sale, too. So, whether or not you like it, you're involved. The sooner we figure this out, the sooner you can be uninvolved."

Rebecca chews on her bottom lip, then walks out of the room without answering.

"Way to go, Jasper," Em says in her best big sister voice.

"Well, it's true."

I chime in with, "You're such a jerk." Then I take a calming breath. "We still need to find someone to decipher the shorthand. I looked it up and I know what some symbols mean, but it's more complicated than that. It would take too long."

Em puts her hand out like we're in class. "I asked Betty from the office. She's got a journalism background. She said she'll be happy to help. So I sent her a few of the pictures you sent me."

"Em!" It's Jasper's turn to be the annoyed sibling. "You can't just give our evidence away! She needs to sign an NDA and..."

I put my hand on his chest. "It's fine...this time."

"Totally," Em agrees.

I flip through several of the pictures, from oldest to newest. "My thing is the handwriting. Yeah, it's shorthand and we can't decipher that right now, but it looks uniform throughout the whole thing. Years...decades. One person writing the exact same way for thirty years? Is that possible?"

Jasper nods. "Yeah, I was thinking about that. The letters we can read, on the names and stuff, are all perfect. Like what you learn in school. Someone went through a lot of trouble to disguise their handwriting."

We all exchange glances.

I'm the first to speak, but barely in a whisper. "You know what that means."

Em answers, "Yeah, no way this is some innocent girl's diary. She'd have to be a hundred years old by now!"

Jasper opens his mouth but doesn't have time to speak because Rebecca walks back into the room.

"Mrs. Adair's maiden name was Hess."

"Mrs. Adair? As in...the blocked off room in the estate sale you said was only a structural issue?" My voice is shrill and I'm trying to control how wide my eyes are. I don't think I'm doing a good job.

"Yes," Rebecca says, sheepishly. "I'm sorry. I couldn't say anything. And you can't say anything now." She looks over her shoulder and lowers her voice. "Nobody knows it's an investigation, yet."

Jasper puts his hands out. "Wait, what? You knew there was a case already?" He's still looking at Rebecca, but that was directed at me.

"No. Of course not. I would have told you. I just...noticed...they had a room cordoned off. But she assured me it was nothing." Again, I try to keep the accusatory tone out of my voice. And again, I think I fail.

"Look," Rebecca says, raising her hands to mirror Jasper's. "We didn't know what it was. She was old, and she died."

"But?" Jasper and I both ask.

"But since she didn't die in the hospital, they sealed the room off just in case."

Em, who had been uncharacteristically quiet until now, asks, "But they let you go on with the estate sale?"

Rebecca nods. "The family insisted, actually. Some probate issue. They had to dissolve most of the estate before—"

"Before they could get their hands on her money," Jasper says with unmasked disgust.

"Welp," Em says, going to the door. "You know what this means."

"Yep," I answer, following her. "We have a case!"

Jasper groans.

"What?" I don't bother turning back, because I know the answer.

"I promised Maura I'd only be here a few minutes. We're supposed to be meeting for dinner later."

"I'm going to the office. What you do is up to you." I don't wait for a reply.

Chase and Eddie come out of the kitchen, but I breeze past them with only a wave.

Eddie asks, "Where are you going?"

And Chase answers for me with, "I know that look."

It's only a ten-minute drive, if that, from Em's new place. The whole time, my mind is reeling about what this all means. Is Mrs. Adair the same E. Hess? I don't know enough about the family. I don't know anything, actually, which is weird in a small town like this. How did they fly under my radar for so long? Could it just be as simple as them not having any kids my age?

I pull into the nearest parking lot and call Chase. I need to know what Mrs. Adair's first name is. Does it start with E? When he doesn't answer, I try Rebecca. She, too, doesn't answer. I'm about to pull back onto the road when the scent of hamburgers wafts by. My stomach reacts swiftly and strongly. I think back through the day and realize I haven't eaten. I've been so consumed with the mystery.

While I'm heading into the Greasy Spoon—no wonder the smell reminded me I'm starving—I send a quick text to Em to see if she's gonna swing by. I don't lure her with the promise of a burger. I know she wants to spend time with Eddie. But I don't want her to show up and not have one for her, just in case.

When my phone buzzes, I'm expecting it to be her, but instead, I get an all caps text from my brother, Ryland. 'GUESS WHAT DAY IT IISSS"

'Not hump day' I reply, then check my lock screen to be sure. Yeah, it's definitely Thursday.

'AirBnB Dayyyy!'

'Do what?'

'I just booked our AirBnB for the trip. You're still coming, right?'

Ohh, the family trip to Lys's. I'd totally forgotten about it. I need to put things on my calendar because these cases consume my every thought. 'Of course. Why aren't you staying with Lys? Save some $$'

'I wouldn't subject anyone to the twins overnight...unless you want to volunteer as a tribute'

I send him back a, '...'

To which, he replies, 'Thought so'

'Can't wait to see everyone, though!'

'What are you up to? Solve any new murders lately?'

I groan. Lys must have unloaded on him about my part-time job. Although, it hasn't felt very part-time lately. 'Maybe'

'Just be safe. I prefer my baby sister alive'

'She also prefers herself that way'

I wait at the door of the Greasy Spoon, but he doesn't answer. Neither has Em.

The smell, which already felt overwhelming in the car, is an assault on my willpower when I step inside. I get a brief flashback of sitting here with Lys during her visit that adds a twinge of missing her to the growing knot of hunger in my stomach.

"Well, if it isn't our very own Sherlock Holmes."

I spin around to see Chris Fanzela, the jerk journalist who keeps dragging me through the mud, coming at me with his hand out. I do not take it. The thought of touching him almost makes me change my mind about eating.

Instead, I turn back toward the takeout counter and order a couple burger and fry combos. I'm sure Em will show up at some point.

"Are you hot on the trail of your next killer, Juniper? What is it this time? A haunted doll? A fancy pen that just so happened to be left beside a dead body?" I hear him take a breath to start up again and I slam my hand down on the counter.

"Or the 'reporter' who ran his mouth too close to a hungry woman?"

That shuts him up and elicits a stifled snort from the teenage girl at the register.

"Is that on the record?"

The girl's brows go up.

"What's your end game here, Chris?"

"Christopher."

"Chris. You harass people in public hoping they won't punch you in the face?"

"Only guilty ones. And I have good insurance." He doesn't sound put off by my threats at all. In fact, I think he's enjoying this.

I take my receipt and step aside, hoping he doesn't follow me but also knowing I'm not that lucky. "Look. I don't know why this stuff keeps happening to me. But I do know, if it was my family member and someone had the chance to help and didn't...I'd be very upset. I'm just trying to help."

"And I'm just trying to understand how all these things started happening in our town now that you're back." The way he emphasizes 'our town' makes it abundantly clear that I'm not included in that 'our.'

The smart thing to do here is keep my mouth shut. "So, in all your journalistic genius, you figured out that I caused Mr. Foster to rob banks twenty years before I was born? Or I caused Olivia's mom to make her life miserable for so long she sought revenge? Or...of course, I planned a car crash in another state to expose my friend for being unfaithful? And for what? To have every item I've received into my shop be confiscated by the police?"

My neck and chest are on fire and I have to grit my teeth to stop the flow of venom that still wants to come out.

Fanzela doesn't waste a second. "All I'm saying is-"

"Junie..." The girl at the register makes eye contact over Fanzela's shoulder. "Your order's ready."

I push past him and give her a grateful smile before taking the brown paper bag.

Who knows how much of that will be plastered across the front page tomorrow? But for now, it feels so good to get it out.

I'll deal with the blowback later.

My jaw is still clenched when I get home and I'm so focused on hating Fanzela, I don't notice the broad shadow darkening my doorstep as I pull in. It's not until I get right up on him and scare both of us that I realize who it is.

His hands are cupped in front of his face, looking in through the large bay window. Beyond both our reflections, my cats are lined up, staring back at Chase.

Ms. Minnie is across the street, standing at her own door, watching intently.

"Am I under investigation?"

He puts his hand over his chest, an innocent and guilty gesture at the same time. "Always."

"I thought you were on a date." I hand him the bag and turn my key in the lock. The door opens and I push it farther with my hip.

"She wants this solved as much as I do. Your shenanigans may have rubbed off on her."

I ignore him and cross the road. "Good afternoon, Ms. Minnie. Hope the cats didn't give you any trouble."

"No, of course not, dear. Angels as always." Her warm smile drifts past me and I think she's looking over my shoulder at the cats until I feel Chase come up behind me.

"I was wondering," I say, giving her a big hug, "What do you know about the Adair family?"

Her sweet expression falters. "That poor woman."

That's not what I expected.

Ms. Minnie rarely needs much prodding to gossip, and now's no exception. "Beth and Ed built that house back in the '30s. They stayed to themselves for a while, but once the kids grew up and started courting...especially when Eddie got married. Oh, it was such a big to do around here. Ed wasn't her first husband, you see, and talk around town was that Little Eddie, their oldest, might not have been his...if you get my drift." The temporary somberness of her tone gave way to near glee as she aired the ancient dirty laundry.

"They had two more after that, a girl and another boy. His mom lived with them for a while, too. Don't know whatever came of her."

Hopefully, the shock doesn't show on my face at the thought of something going on in this town flying under Ms. Minnie's radar.

"After the kids moved off, they didn't get out much. She stopped going to council meetings and my James said Ed quit the poker game. Rather abruptly, too, if I recall right." Her wrinkled hand goes over her mouth and she gets that faraway look in her eyes.

"What council?" I ask, hoping to bring her back to the present.

"Ladies Council, of course."

"*The* Ladies Council? Of Landrum?"

"Is there any other?"

"No, suppose not. It's just...I'm—well, I'm not really *on* the Council, I guess. But I've been making blankets. A blanket," I stammer.

"That's so nice of you, dear. They could use all the help they can get. But yeah," she says, coming back around, "they stopped going out. Nobody saw hide nor hair of 'em for years. Then Ed died...that was about three years ago, right Sheriff?"

Chase makes a noise that tells me he doesn't want to talk about the case, but also knows better than to not answer Ms. Minnie when she speaks. "Yes, ma'am, I think that's about right."

"Hmm," I add. "That's weird. I thought-" Chase grabs my arm to cut me off, and it works.

Miss Minnie looks up at him and, with the most innocent expression, asks, "How's Becky doing these days?"

The air rushes out of Chase and he turns beet red, then bolts back across the street.

Ms. Minnie smiles at me and we both stifle a laugh.

I'm about to follow him when Ms. Minnie says, "I wonder whatever happened to Ms. Eileen."

Chapter Ten

Friday

I stifle a yawn, hoping the nice young woman in my shop doesn't notice. It's not her fault—though she has been wandering around aimlessly for a good fifteen minutes and refused my help twice. No, I'm exhausted because I stayed up way past my bedtime last night, recreating the diary.

My behavior had rattled the cats, who also got up and stood guard around me and the coffee table. It's a good thing I recently came across a bunch of new books to stack under it, or my back would be killing me right now. We're all paying for it today, but it had to be done.

The odds of Chase giving me back the diary any time soon are close to zero. My only choice was to copy it into one of my many, many empty notebooks. It's always so hard deciding what's worth marking up that first clean page. But if this doesn't make the cut, nothing ever will.

Considering I only have less than half of the pages recorded, it shouldn't have taken as long as it did. But I was so fascinated by the author's attention to detail, I couldn't rush through it. I did, however, give up trying to copy the perfect letting after a couple of pages. That was brutal. I don't know how they did it for years.

My internal alarm goes off when the woman gets close to my typewriters. I'm still a little sore from having to sell the Blick. I can't take another hit so soon. I leave my post behind the counter. I'm pretty sure I won't need my panic button right now. This woman's not as big as Typewriter Guy, and nowhere near as big as Almost Lamp Guy.

I wonder what he was really looking for. That strange noise that keeps happening interrupted us and he ended up not buying anything. I hope he comes back...*for sales purposes only*, I tell myself.

Her dress is a lovely patchwork of flowers on a dark blue background, my perfect in. "Did you see the Bristow landscape over here? She's one of my favorites. They have such a dreamy quality." I motion toward the wall to my right, away from my typewriters.

This time, the woman is receptive to my sales charm and begins admiring the wall of art. What actually catches her eye is a Dutch-style oil painting of an old man with a pipe. There's at least a century of grime covering it, making the man and the background look gray-washed. "I like him," she says after a moment.

"Yes, there's something about him, isn't there? I came across this one at an estate sale in Pennsylvania a few years ago."

"You went all the way to Pennsylvania for-"

"Oh, no!" I laugh. "I was already there. Could you imagine?" Although, I can and do imagine that a lot. Traveling the world chasing the high of finding the perfect piece for my collection...which is now my shop.

"He reminds me of my grandfather." The words come out slowly, almost reluctantly.

"Yes, I suppose he has that air about him. I think that's why I never had it restored. He feels more alive this way." I run my fingers along the bottom of the man's shirt, feeling the built up paint of a sleeve crease before it disappears into the frame. "This is my favorite part, right here."

The woman does not reach out a hand to caress the painting and I pull mine back, embarrassed. She doesn't seem to fault me for it, though. "How much?"

I tell her. It's a fair price, not as high as I could go, but higher than I would have in the past. I think I'm starting to get the hang of Lys's 'You have a store to sell things, not give them away' idea.

She doesn't seem put off by the number. Instead, she nods and begins digging in her thin black clutch for her card. I have a brief, odd thought. Her purse looks like it's worth more than the painting. But it's overshadowed by the thrill of the sale, and I hurry to the counter.

"Do you deliver?"

I've already charged her and wrapped the painting. "Um..." My first thought is Rusty delivering my paintings and what happened next. The idea of going around to strangers' houses doesn't appeal to me much anymore, but it seems delivery is the name of the game these days. "Sure. Just write your address down for me and I'll get it over to you ASAP."

"Thanks. I really appreciate it. I hadn't planned on buying anything so big. I actually came here looking for something..." Her voice trails off.

I pull a yellow sticky note out from under the counter and pass it to her. "Well, if you're in the market for something specific, let me know and I'll keep an eye out. I'm always stumbling across peculiar things."

"Really? What's the most recent peculiar thing you stumbled upon?" She doesn't look up from writing her name and address on the sticky note.

The obvious answer is the diary falling out of the desk, but I can't say that. Even if it wasn't part of a police investigation already, I could never imagine selling it. "A couple months ago, I got a doll with human hair," I almost whisper. Then, "Wanna see it?" I do *not* whisper.

"No!" Her answer comes faster than I can finish the question.

"Yeah," I say with a low chuckle. "That's why I keep her over there." I point to a far corner to my left, where the more curious items are kept.

"Well, good luck with that," she says as she's heading toward the door. "Stay safe."

I smile at her back as I walk with her. People our age aren't usually superstitious, but now and then you find one. "Always. I'll call you when I get ready to deliver, probably tomorrow, Ms...." I forgot to look at the sticky note. Lys would kill me if she were here. Not learning a customer's name is a rookie mistake.

"Jansen. Thank you."

When she's gone, I twist the sign over to Closed. Another thing Lys would be livid about, but I have more important things to concern myself with.

Sir Fluffington III

Sir Fluffington III waits by the door. Miss Junie and the woman in the flower dress are talking, so it should be easy enough to run out when the door opens. He doesn't like subterfuge, but he also doesn't want to be saddled with the kids right now. He needs time to himself.

Maybe it's that darn noise driving him crazy. No matter how many times he hears it, he can't find where it's coming from. It's just a low, grumbling creak that sounds like it comes from everywhere and nowhere all at once. How's he supposed to command his subordinates to take care of the issue when he still doesn't know what the issue is?

He shakes his head, clearing out the echoes of the noise.

Yes, what he needs is some peace and quiet. Just for a little while.

He gave Spot and Sassafras jobs to do, ones that would take them both down to the basement office and away from his side. He should feel guilty about it. He doesn't really care what's happening in the little mouse hole Mr. Jasper found a couple of weeks ago. The time for caring was then, not now. But they seemed all too eager to jump on the task, so he let them.

No, he doesn't feel guilty about that part at all. The thing pulling at his conscience is leaving Miss Junie unattended. With Spot and Sassafras in the basement, her safety is his responsibility. But he rationalizes the guilt away by remembering that Mr. Chase and Mr. Jasper installed that panic button under the table for her. Well, some of the guilt. The rest he will carry with him until he returns.

When the door finally opens, Sir Fluffington III makes a run for it, across the side yard and down the street. He's at the stop sign before he dares to look back. He's relieved to find that he has not been followed. Slowing his pace, he let his feet take him wherever they wish.

Juniper

"Was that Fluff?" I say out loud to myself? Weird, I haven't seen him leave the house without the other two cats in forever.

I walk through the shop and into my apartment. The notebook where I started copying the diary pages is on my coffee table, beckoning me. I force myself to go into the kitchen and make a cup of tea first.

Em brought me something called Thai iced tea from one of her reviews, and I've been trying to recreate it ever since. This batch is the closest I've come yet, but there's still something missing. The one she found had a pleasant, tingling flavor that reminded me of my childhood. I just haven't been able to figure it out. Still, as I take the first sip of my latest concoction, it's divine.

My phone buzzes in my pocket and I figure it's Em or Jasper. I sent them both pictures of my handiwork this morning. Em's been getting up earlier now that she's a corporate baddie, but I know not to expect anything from her before ten. Awake and conscious are two different things.

I set the tea down on the far end of the glass coffee table, remembering the catastrophe with Lys and the Erasmus. Mr. G still hasn't been able to get the stain out. I couldn't imagine spilling this orange tea all over my hard work.

When my phone buzzes again with the reminder, I pull it out and see it was actually a phone call from Em, not a text. That's unusual.

I call her back, my mind already spinning with a million bad scenarios.

"Hey! Those look outstanding! Did you do that yourself?" She doesn't waste any time with pleasantries.

"Wha-Oh, the diary? Yeah. It's hard work. Whoever did this was very dedicated. My hand's gonna be sore for days, I can tell. And I'm not even halfway through the stuff I have. Not to mention everything that's missing. I-"

I stop. There's a familiar sound coming from her end of the phone and it's taken this long for my brain to catch up and recognize it.

"Have you-"

"Shhh!"

"Huh?"

"Shhh!" I listen carefully for a moment to be sure. Then I squeal in her ear. "Are you watching Ex Island without me?"

"What? No! Well...not really. This is season one. I'm restarting it to show Eddie." There's a rustling sound, like she's covering the phone with her hand. Then she whispers, "He thinks Sarah and Mikey C are meant for each other."

We both giggle. I remember rooting for Sarah and Mikey C, too, only to be heartbroken when she went back with Blaine. Just the thought of his smug face at the reunion makes me want to punch something.

"Well, don't tell him! And we need to catch up on this season. I've been avoiding social media for weeks!"

"I know. I promise I'll get over there soon and we can have a girls' night in. Oh, and the real reason I called was to tell you Betty should have the first batch of notes transcribed this afternoon or tomorrow at the latest. She said she'd let me know."

"That's good. I had so much trouble copying the shorthand. I'm sure I got it very wrong. So I'm glad I got at least some of it on video." I look over at my notebook, my fingers itching to get back to it. "Oh! I made another pitcher of that tea. I'm getting so close!"

Em laughs. "You're like a mad scientist all of a sudden."

"Your fault!"

"Don't get too carried away and forget what's really important. This case!"

I can't help the smile that forms on my lips. If it was Lys on the other end of the phone, I'd be getting a lecture about fiscal responsibility and keeping my mind on the shop. But Em knows me so well. Until we figure out this mystery, it's going to consume me. "Yeah, I'm about to talk to Jasper about the names in the book. There's a definite pattern. I just have to find it."

"Well, I'll leave you to that. I'm gonna go watch Eddie watch Ex Island. Ask Jasper if he wants to meet for lunch later. Might be the only way I drag myself out of this house today. And same for you. Don't sit hunched over that notebook all day."

"I wasn't hunched," I lie.

After we hang up, I immediately dial Jasper's number. Might as well get this over with.

He picks up before the first ring, somehow. "Hey, I was just about to call you."

"Cool. What for?"

"I'm hungry. And I figure if we meet up to talk about the case...it's a write-off."

I roll my eyes, though he can't see it. "You are your sister's brother."

"Yeah, that's usually how that works."

"I just got off the phone with her and she wanted me to set up lunch for us. I guess you're buying, then."

"Sure, but only if you bring the notebook."

"I'm not leaving without it. But it'll be at least an hour. She's finishing up some stuff and I want to get one more page copied before I go."

There's a quick pause, then a loud sigh. "Fine. I guess I can eat some chips. I'll text the group about where we're going...since I'm paying."

"Good idea," I say, not taking his bait. "We can use this business meeting to divvy up the tasks. Em's making progress on the shorthand. Can't let your big sister show you up on your own case, can we?"

"I'm checking out the Adair family already. But the sooner we get to lunch, the sooner we can crack this case."

I hang up and finally settle in to finish the diary pages. I'm not gonna lie. As motivated as I was before to solve this strange puzzle, a race to beat Jasper—and yes, Em—has my fingers flying across the page.

Chapter Eleven

"Figures," I tell Em as we wait outside Good Thymes, a new vegan restaurant where the old car wash used to be. "Making me eat vegetables *and* not even show up on time."

"I'm with him on the vegetables thing, but yeah, I'm not standing out here much longer." She bounces from one leg to the other and, considering how I have to look up to meet her eyes, I know she's wearing those impossible boots again.

"How far did you get on Ex Island?"

"Only one more episode. He still thinks they're the end game. I'm feeling bad about how much I can't wait for him to find out." Em looks at her phone and I do the same. Nothing from Jasper.

"Let's just go in." I pull up our group chat and text him we're done waiting, as if I'm dying to get ahold of some vegetables.

Unfortunately, when we step inside, the place smells delicious. It's nothing like I'd expect from a vegan place, although I have no frame of reference, either. I take a big sniff, trying to discern all the different spices and oils. If the food tastes half as good as it smells, I might have a new favorite. I'm feeling rather adventurous just being here, considering my go-to is still chicken nuggets.

Speaking of adventurous, "Is he springing Maura on me again?"

"Huh?" Em holds up three fingers for the host and he shows us to our table.

"Better only be three," I say, not very under my breath.

We order our drinks—I'm in the mood for lemonade—and a water for Jasper. "I don't think he'd spring her on you," Em finally answers.

I make a clear not-buying-it face. "How else does he know about a vegan restaurant?"

Her brow scrunches. "Is Maura vegan?"

"How should I know? She's *your* sister-in-law."

"Whoa!" Jasper suddenly appears over us. "Let's not get ahead of ourselves." He takes the seat beside Em. I hold my breath and, thankfully, Maura doesn't take the one in front of me.

"Made you look," he says in an annoying tone that reminds me too much of the bratty little kid we had a hard time getting rid of.

"So why here?"

"Did you bring your notebook?"

I pull it out of my bag and place it on the table.

"Does the name B. Abbott ring a bell?"

I shrug. When I first started filling out the notebook, I tried memorizing the names. But I've copied so many, they all run together.

Jasper flips through until he finds what he's looking for, then jabs his finger onto the page. "B. Abbott, March 22, 1994, 12:48-15:22." Then he cuts his eyes over to a young woman wiping down a counter.

She's short and cheery, and way too young to be in a book from the '90s.

Jasper must sense the objection waiting on my lips. "Ladies, meet Trixie Abbott, short for Beatrice...her grandmother."

It doesn't need to be said, but I say it anyway. "B. Abbott."

"What...happened to B. Abbott?" Em asks. It's the first words she's spoken since he got here. I wonder if she was letting us duke it out, so she didn't have to get involved.

Jasper throws his hands up and leans back in his seat. "Dunno. Whatever happened, it was in the missing pages."

I look up at the smiling brunette girl and frown. "Well, we can't just go ask her."

"But you know who we can ask?" Jasper leans back toward me. "Chase."

Before I can argue—about not grilling Chase, and about him refusing to give me information anyway—the sweet, young girl in question comes by to take our orders.

"Hi! I'm Trixie. I'll be guiding you through your culinary experience today. I would normally ask if you've been here before, but seeing as how this is our grand opening week, probably not."

We all smile at her and I try to fix my face so the sadness and fear doesn't shine through. I bet we look so creepy right now. "No," I say when nobody else does. "I haven't been here. And, honestly, vegetables scare me. So you've got your work cut out for you."

Trixie laughs, a bright and airy sound that makes me hope I don't see an octagon next to B. Abbott when we get the diary back. I've seen a couple of red ones so far in my transcribing and I think it means what I don't want it to mean.

"Don't worry. Some of these recipes are handed down for generations. We've had plenty of time to perfect them."

I don't ask the question I'm dying to ask. Instead, I say, "We?"

Her smile widens, as if that were possible. "Yes! My mom's side of the family has been vegan for...ever. This has been her dream for a long time and now she's finally doing it. I'm so proud of her."

I do some quick math in my head. If it's her mom's side of the family, that doesn't tell us anything, since B. Abbott would be her paternal grandmother.

Em takes up the slack from my silence. "Well, it all smells so wonderful. What do you suggest?"

"Personally, I love the black bean enchiladas. She won't tell me what she does with the red sauce, but I could drink the stuff!"

"I'm sold!" Em closes her menu.

Jasper closes his menu as well. "I'll have the stir fry. And our friend here will have the nuggets."

I gasp. "Nuggets?" He points to the flip side of my menu. "Wow. I have to try the nuggets."

"Perfect! I'll get that right in."

We hand our menus to Trixie and watch her go.

I chew on my bottom lip. "I really hope her grandmother's alright."

"Me, too." Em says. "How did you find her?"

Jasper takes his phone out of his pocket and swipes away several notifications. With each one, his smile turns to a frown, then a scowl.

Remind me again why I need a love life? I smirk to myself.

"I was looking up some of the names at the library and found the notice for this restaurant opening." He gives Em a smug look.

"Yes, I knew this place existed. Obviously. But I'm under strict orders to have my underlings do local spots. I'm in the big time now, baby." She says the last part with that mocking tone she gets when she's repeating some of Harry's favorite sayings. And this is definitely one he's been trying to get through her head since she took the promotion. "Besides, the name wouldn't have stuck out to me, anyway. *You're* the detective in the family."

"So, what do we do now?" I ask as a way to break them up before things get out of hand. They have a tendency to go from zero to a million in a flash.

"We do more research. And we get info out of Chase."

Dang. I'd hoped he'd forgotten about that part. "I doubt he'll give me anything, but I'll try. He didn't answer earlier. And really, this is more of an in-person begging situation. I can't tomorrow, probably. I'm delivering that painting. So-"

"You're what?" Em interrupts.

"I sold the old dutchman. She didn't have her car, so I said I'd deliver it tomorrow." I shrug to show them it's no big deal, though I can already see the looks on their faces turning sour.

Em's the first to shake her head. "Absolutely not. Haven't you learned anything?"

"I said '*she*.'" I emphasize the word and drag it out.

"No," Jasper adds. "I agree with Em."

"Oh, so *now* you two agree? Go figure. Stop being paranoid." My attitude is getting the best of me. Wasn't I just thinking these exact same things back at my shop?

Jasper waves a hand over the table to shush us as Trixie delivers our food. The nuggets look exactly like chicken. I actually want to dig in...to vegetables. Is this what growing up feels like?

After Trixie tells us to 'dig in,' and hurries over to the next table, Jasper holds up his phone again. "Let's table the painting fight for now. What I wanted to show you earlier was-" He swipes away more notifications. "I found someone, a reporter. They seem to have been on the trail of something, but then their articles stopped suddenly."

Em says, "No."

And I say, "Wow," at the same time. "So…is the reporter the author of the diary? Or one of the entries?" It takes everything I have not to say 'victims' instead. We're still not totally there yet.

Are we?

Then, for some unknown reason, the hairs standing on the back of my neck right now remind me of all the times it's been happening recently and I blurt out, "There's a weird noise at my house."

Obviously, that catches them off guard and they both stare at me.

"I don't know why, but that reminded me. I can't find it. But it's been going on for weeks. It's driving me crazy. And the cats."

"What kind of noise?" Jasper asks.

I try my best to explain the low creaking, crackling, grumbling sound, but to no avail. "I don't know. You have to hear it for yourself."

Then I realize, as much as Jasper's at the shop, down in the office, why hasn't he heard it?

I'm about to say the unthinkable—that it not happening when he's there is on purpose—when his phone dings.

He grumbles, way closer to the sound the noise makes than I could get. "Maura and I had plans to go to that ax throwing place on Poplar, but she had a meeting and it's too late to cancel. You guys wanna go?"

Em and I exchange evil grins.

"See, told you. It says right here, specifically, that you won't kill your little brother with their company axes." Jasper says, pointing to the liability waiver on the window of Lumberjax.

Em shrugs. "That's fine. I'll just have Junie do it." She pushes past him and walks in.

Jasper eyes me before making a show of chivalrously holding the door and waving me in.

"It's a start," I say with a royal nod.

The place is a lot quieter than I expect, with only the occasional thwump of an ax hitting a target. The rest of the sounds are the usual din of a restaurant or sports bar. The smell of wood is everywhere, and somehow relaxing.

"So," I say to Jasper after he shows his reservation email to the guy at the counter. "Is this now a write-off, too?"

He actually thinks for a moment, then answers. "Only if we interview a potential client or witness...or suspect." He adds the last part with a wry smile and raised eyebrow.

I look around at all the people holding axes. "Let's hope not."

Em slides her arm through mine and pulls me toward a booth. It looks like a very serious dart competition, with a long wooden corridor and a bullseye painted on a wall far away. A row of axes line the sides like pool sticks and I stare at them, wondering how in the world you're supposed to choose one.

"I think it's by weight."

I haven't had time to register that this isn't Jasper's voice before an enormous shadow fills the small space. I turn to find the customer from my shop standing rather close behind me. It's unnerving for several reasons, one of which is the gorgeous brunette at his side.

"Oh, um, have you...axed...before?"

He and his beautiful companion exchange unreadable glances, then he smiles widely in my direction. "You could say that." Without asking, he reaches across me and takes the largest ax off the wall. Then, in what looks like an effortless flick of his wrist, the tip buries itself deep into the bullseye at the end of our lane.

The woman he's with rolls her eyes. "Please excuse my brother. One of these places popped up near his house and he spends way too much time there."

Brother? She looks old enough to be his mother, but still gorgeous enough I thought she was his date. Brother and sister? That never would have registered.

Em catches my eye over her shoulder. Well, more like Em waves frantically until I have no choice but to acknowledge her. Then she mouths, "Sister!"

"Impressive," I say to the man, whose name I still don't know. All I remember is the piercing blue eyes and thick beard, both of which are still quite unnerving. "Although, I think that's my point. Or..." I squint to read the target. "Fifty points."

The woman, his sister, sticks out her hand. "Since he's too rude to do it, I'm Francine."

I take her hand. "Hi, Francine. Junie. This is Emerald and Jasper. And..." I look back up at her brother towering over me. "Don't take it too hard. He never told me his own name."

She groans and smacks him on the arm. Yep, definitely siblings. "Roger! Really? You come invade these people's space and they don't even know who you are?"

He shrugs, more like one would to shoo a fly than from embarrassment. "She knows who I am. Junie's the one I told you about. With the antique shop."

My phone buzzes, but I ignore it. Then Em's waving again and pointing down at my phone. I back up a smidge, which is really all the room I have, and glance at the screen.

'OMG he's cute! And he told his sister about you! Which one is he? Typewriter Guy or Lamp Guy?'

My cheeks burn, but I type back a quick, '2nd'

"So," Almost Lamp Guy—Roger—says, "did you ever find that weird noise?" He leans in toward his sister. "I didn't actually get to buy anything because we got interrupted." Then, back in my direction, "I promise to come back soon and finish the sale."

I nod.

"Well," Francine tugs on his shirtsleeve. "Let's leave these nice people to their ax throwing. The last thing they need is distractions."

"Of course." Roger let her lead him out the door.

Jasper stands perfectly still, dumbfounded, while Em squeals.

I turn back to the row of axes. "Who's up next?"

"Oh, no you don't." Em pulls me back to face her. "Tell me everything you know about him."

"Nothing! You were standing right there when I just learned his name. He's a customer, and that's it. Not even that, because, as you also heard, he never bought anything."

"Yet," she answers with a wink.

Jasper finally speaks up, but doesn't help at all. "What do you know about him?"

"What? Et tu, Jasper?"

He waves me off. "I don't care if you like him. I care who he is. That's the guy I saw leaving the shop the other day, right?"

I shrug. "Guess so."

"Alright. And I told Maura I had a bad feeling about him. And now he's here, where you are?"

"First off," I say, folding my arms and planting my feet. "Your 'bad feelings' aren't trustworthy. Or else you'd have them *about* Maura.

And second, I wasn't supposed to be here. So bumping into each other was totally random."

He doesn't budge. "I'm just saying. You've had killers show up at your shop before."

"Ugh!" I throw my hands up. "Is that what this is about? You trying to turn this into a write-off?"

He's quiet for a second, not denying the accusation. Then, almost as an afterthought, he adds, "Technically, we're talking about the case right now, so it's already a write-off. And I still don't trust the guy."

Em steps between us. "I, for one, am glad we came here. Junie, you didn't tell me he was so cute!"

"He's not. He's a potential customer. That's all I see."

"Mm-hmm." She makes a fawning face, batting her eyes, then, in a mimicking tone, repeats my own words. "He never told me his own name."

I give her a playful shove. "I did not sound like that."

Jasper comes to her defense. "You kinda did."

"Yep," Em says in her own voice again. "Downright giddy."

I shake my head. "You guys remember we're standing by a lot of axes, right?"

"Yeah," Jasper says, "And I don't like how good your new killer boyfriend is at throwing them."

Chapter Twelve

SIR FLUFFINGTON III

Sir Fluffington III watches the herd of young children chasing the ice cream truck down Randolph Avenue. When he was a younger cat, he'd lay in wait at the corner, sure at least one would drop a treat for him. He spies one such opportunist crouching in a bush, bright orange eyes darting back and forth.

Those were the good old days.

He has half a mind to wait around and watch the hunt unfold, but he's on a mission, whether or not he'll admit it to himself.

Miss Junie has gotten herself mixed up in some dangerous situations lately, and Sir Fluffington III can't help but worry that this new one will be the worst of them all. He's overheard several conversations between her and Mr. Jasper about the diary. From context, he now knows that the word means a book that you write secrets in.

That's never good.

Sir Fluffington III knows all too well what he's done to protect his own secrets in the past. Not that it worked.

He shakes his head to dispel the image of Mariel walking out of his life for good.

He also ignores the fact that his feet are taking him back to the place where it happened. He thought, after running into Tank at the old pool, he'd gotten closure. But seeing her, instead of Duke, waiting for him that day...it all came rushing back.

The gravel under his paws let him know he's arrived. He peers over the edge of the road to check how high the water's gotten since his last visit. Surprisingly, it's lower than expected. With a sniff of the air, he can tell it's been this way for a while.

Up ahead, the long red building stretches across the bridge to the other side. His first time here, he thought it was a house. It looks like one, just with no back wall. It was rather disorienting back then, as well. But now, he finds comfort in thinking about how many people—and animals—have passed through this makeshift building.

As he inches closer, he turns his head to the side, examining the way the whole thing slants to the right. That, too, seems to have changed over the years. If he were a younger cat, he might bound across the bridge without a care. But in his wise old age, he knows to take it slow. Another whiff brings with it the powerful scent of paint, and he notices several bright red spots that look fresh. At least someone's taking care of the place.

He hasn't crossed the bridge since before that day, long ago. The day he was too scared to cross over into the unknown... with her.

Now, as he stands at the entrance as he did then, he can almost picture her there, on the other side. Her sad tail swishing in the summer heat. Her ears down, then up, and down again when she must have realized he was not crossing with her.

"Fluffy?" He can almost hear her voice the same as- "Fluff?"

Sir Fluffington III blinks.

"Mariel?"

"What are you doing here?" She stands perfectly still for a moment. Then, as he had silently begged her to do all those years ago, she crosses back over to him.

They circle each other and he wonders if she, too, thinks he's just a mirage.

"I-" He should say he was hoping he'd find her here, but he's not ready to admit that to either of them. Instead, he puffs his chest and says the exact wrong thing. "I was looking for clues."

Juniper

I'm awakened in the night by a scratching sound. My first thought is Peep got stuck somewhere. I hurry out to the kitchen and turn on the light to find him in the middle of the floor. He scurries back to his little house, but not before a quick glance in my direction. If I didn't know any better, I'd say that glance translates to 'Good, you handle it.'

And by 'it,' I now know is the whining, wailing cat outside the back door.

There are several more scratches before I can wrestle it open. Fluff is waiting, paws furiously in the air, for another attack on my door. His mouth is wide open for another meow.

"What on Earth?"

He trots in as if he hadn't just made a terrible scene in the middle of the night. I look around to see if any of the neighboring lights have turned on. For once, I'm glad I live on a mostly retail street. There's nobody to hear him scream.

With a shiver, I hope the same won't apply to me someday.

Fluff marches past me, goes straight to the room, and hops up on my side of the bed. Spot and Sass pop their heads up long enough to watch him make one circle, knead my blanket a couple times, then plop down.

My mouth is still open, planning to lecture him about not coming home when the streetlights turn on, or any of the other things my mom would say to us growing up. But it's clear my words would fall on deaf ears. I pull as much of the blanket as I can from under him and scooch onto a sliver of the bed. There's an entire half of it open over there, but this is my side. I'm not giving it up without a fight.

Although I know it was just Fluff coming home, my ears are still perked, listening for any new or unusual sounds while I lay here waiting for my heartbeat to settle. I'm getting used to the strange noise now, enough to almost expect it and get a jump on tracking it down.

That's what I'm concentrating on when another, more shrill sound startles all of us. It takes even longer for me to place it, because it's not one I ever hear.

The telephone in the shop, that never rings, is ringing now.

"See what you did," I grumble to Fluff as I climb out of bed to answer it. I'm rehearsing my apology as I head to the shop.

I pick up the receiver and start my spiel. "Hello? I'm so sor-"

"Is this Juniper's Jewels?" The voice of an old, frail woman comes through the phone. I get an instant image of someone hunched over a knitting project in a rocking chair. Someone who has no business being awake at this hour.

"Uh, yes. I'm sorry for the noise. My cat-"

"Your what, dear? I'm not calling about a cat."

"Oh?"

"I'm sorry to call so early..."

Early?

I look at one of my many large wall clocks to see that it's just after five.

Fluff was out all night.

"...a desk I've been looking for."

"A what? I-I'm sorry." I yawn and try to let my breath out slowly. "A desk?"

"Yes." Her voice doesn't sound as old and feeble now that she's onto what she wants. "I saw in the paper here that you just purchased a roller desk from-"

"The paper?"

Fanzela!

How did he know about the desk? I start to walk out the front door to grab my copy of the paper, but the phone cord yanks me back in. How did people live being tethered to the wall like this?

"Do you still have it? I can send someone by today to pick it up. Whatever price you want. Name it."

"I'm sorry. I'm not selling it—a roller desk. I got one, yes. But it's not for sale. I do have-"

The line goes dead.

Chapter Thirteen

September 16, 2023

Saturday

"Spot! Go get Fluff up. This isn't fair!" I groan as I turn the Closed sign to Open. It feels like I've already worked an entire day and everyone else is just getting started. Of course, I peek through the window to see Ms. Minnie whistling and humming as she sets out her fresh flowers. She looks like she's been up even longer and loved every second.

I step away before she sees me. I love her and all, but I'm not ready for people.

"Fluff!" I call back toward the apartment. "If I have to be up, so do you!"

Spot comes slinking back into the shop without Fluff. I bend down and give him a good scratch behind the ears. "It's OK, buddy. I know you did your best."

Sass meows at me and I scratch her, too. But she pulls away. She's looking toward the apartment and I'm now sure that meow meant, "Let me try."

I'm sure she could definitely get him up, but at what cost? There isn't room for two grumps in the shop today. "Let him sleep. I'm sure whatever he was doing last night was very important."

Honestly, I should thank him. I made a lot of progress on the diary. I'm almost done with what I have recorded. The problem is, it doesn't look good.

If what I'm seeing is true, a lot of the names in this diary are of dead people. Ones who weren't dead before they showed up in this diary.

I haven't been able to find much on B. Abbott. Whoever wrote this diary was smart enough to only use first initials. There are so many people, alive and dead, with that mix of initial and name. The main one all over Google right now is Trixie. I smile, remembering her bubbly personality and how it shined through all the newspaper articles about the restaurant. She's quickly become the spunky little face of the vegan movement in Landrum, SC. Not that I even knew before yesterday that there was one.

Aside from still copying the diary entries from my video, I've also started a second notebook for tracking names of possible victims. It's filling up fast. Too fast. I already sacrificed one pen to the cause, and now, the one in my hand isn't faring too well, either.

Could there really be a serial killer in Landrum that went unnoticed for decades? Or was this the diary of a journalist following a serial killer? I'm still not sure. I don't even know if every one of these people died here, or under suspicious circumstances. There's so much to keep track of. Maybe I need a third notebook!

That might not be a bad idea, though. I keep drawing the symbols and scratching them out when I change my mind about what they mean. The only one I'm fairly sure about is the octagon. The Ominous Octagon is what I've been calling it. It's become glaringly obvious that whenever I see one beside a person's name, they will no longer appear in the diary.

Even worse, an increasing number of them are colored in...red. If that doesn't mean bloody murder, I don't know what does.

I know I've been up too long and running on little sleep, so I try to infuse a little logic into my theories. A red octagon is a stop sign. So, innocently enough, it could mean that the author of the diary *stopped* following the person. Unfortunately, I've yet to find a red octagon next to a name that didn't have an obituary.

Although, maybe fortunately, the limited research I've been able to do so far turned up several people who died of apparently natural causes. Does that mean this diary really belonged to a journalist who was tracking mysterious natural deaths that might not be natural after all? Or could it be someone who knows how to make deaths look natural?

This is so mind-boggling. It's days like today I wish I hadn't kicked my coffee habit.

I put down the pen and stretch my fingers, then the rest of me. When I look back at the clock, I realize I've already been sitting here an hour. It's time for caffeine.

As I'm in the kitchen, making the last bit of my latest Thai tea concoction, I notice Fluff finally getting out of the bed. His yawn and stretch causes me to do the same again. "You're a bad influence."

I chug the tea and start to make a new pitcher when my phone buzzes. It's the alarm I set to remind me to take the painting over to Miss Jansen. A creepy feeling crawls up my spine as I remember the conversation I had with Em and Jasper yesterday, but I push it down and head back into the shop.

The concern for my safety is quickly replaced by a more urgent feeling of irritation. I never finished wrapping the painting. I quickly grab the nearest wad of recycled paper and start taping it to the back and the frame. I'm not sure how much to use, so I keep going until the paper feels like enough cushion to save the painting if, or when, I trip over my own two feet and drop it.

"That should do it."

I hold the painting up for the cat to admire my handiwork, but they seem more interested in the leftover paper on the floor. I surreptitiously drop another few scraps as I am walking towards the front door. "Everybody, please behave while I'm gone. I'm too tired for more shenanigans than I already have."

Spot and Sass are too busy playing with the paper to acknowledge me. Fluff, on the other hand, is sitting on top of the 18th century armoire, watching the festivities. He gives me a quick answering meow, which neither confirms nor denies that he will behave.

As I lock the door behind me on my way to personally deliver the painting Em and Jasper asked me not to deliver by myself. I figure it's the best non-answer I can hope for.

After struggling, and failing, to fit the painting in my trunk, I regroup and place it carefully in the backseat. The painting itself is barely larger than a sheet of paper, plus the ornate frame. I consider this a true testament to my ability to not clean my car out.

Although, now that the shop is more empty than it's ever been, I suppose I have no excuse. Unless I come up with another one fast, I see a day of organizing in my future.

Maybe Em and Jasper are onto something and Ms. Jansen will kill me before I have to un-hoard my life again.

I laugh, punch the address into my phone, and start the car. The woman was so lovely yesterday. The odds of her killing me are very low. Still, if this new part-time job has taught me anything, low isn't zero. I call Jasper on my way.

"Are you in your car?"

"Yeah, I'm on the way to deliver the painting. Stay on the line with me."

There's a heavy sigh that ends in a low groan. "Junie, this isn't the same as not delivering it alone. You were supposed to get someone to go with you."

"No, that's what you *told* me to do. Next time...don't."

"So, you're willing to get yourself killed to prove a point?"

"She's not gonna kill me. She was very sweet." I ply him with the same rationalization I gave myself.

"Ha! You should see all the sweet old ladies I come across in my investigations who absolutely would kill you."

"Good thing she's young." I follow the GPS instructions and turn down Rutherford. "Oh."

"Oh, what?"

"Nothing."

"Juniper."

I stall for a moment, talking to the car in front of me about going so slow, instead of coming clean.

"Junie!"

"It's fine."

There's a scratching, fumbling sound, then a whisper. The next thing I hear is Em. "What are you doing?"

I freeze. "What are *you* doing?"

"Getting ready for lunch. What's going on?" She has her boss' voice on, and it almost works.

"You're going to lunch without me?"

"With Maura..." She lets that sink in before adding, "Now what's going on?"

Now I really want to take my frustrations out on the slow car in front of me. "Like I told your traitor brother...nothing. I just realized the address the painting lady gave me is close to the Adair's house."

"Do. Not. Go. Over. There."

"Sorry, gotta go. I'm about to pull in." I'm not, but I hang up anyway. I wasn't planning ongoing by there—not really—but now I am.

Five minutes later, I arrive at the address for Ms. Jansen. My phone has been going off like crazy, but I don't bother answering. I do, however, shove it in my pocket as I take the painting up to the house.

It's a cute little cottage style, something I'm more used to seeing around town. It sets me at ease. The flowers, bushes full of pinks and purples, remind me again of the cute dress she had on yesterday. I ring the bell and wait, taking in the scent of the flowers and a hint of paint. I look around to see a fresh white coat on the door and around the windowpanes.

The door in question opens and I'm greeted by a paint and dust covered woman with a bright smile. "Oh! Perfect!" Ms. Jansen waves me in. "Sorry, I'm remodeling."

"Wow," I say, and mean it. The inside of the house is gutted, but still surprisingly homey. The warm yellow lighting in the small foyer draws your eyes to the open living and dining room, which also has a fresh coat of paint. The pale blue reminds me, yet again, of her pretty dress. The paintings and knick-knacks huddled in the corner are an abundance of flowers in every color.

I'm noticing a pattern. Then I remember the painting in my hand, one that doesn't match this decor at all.

She must see my confused expression, because she takes my arm and leads me farther into the house. "That's going in here." She opens a dark brown door, revealing an untouched, musty old library. "My grandfather's study. This was his house. It's mine now, but this...I can't imagine changing one thing. Aside from this lovely painting. Look."

She goes deeper into the room and picks up a small framed picture off the long wooden desk. When she turns it around, I see why she fell in love with my Dutch man so much. The picture of the man, which I assume is her grandfather, looks almost exactly like the painting, down to the grizzled look on both their faces.

"It's uncanny," I say, reaching out to touch the picture.

"I know, right? That's why I just had to have it."

Part of me feels guilty for charging as much as I did for the painting, though it's well worth a lot more. I'm about to renegotiate the price in her favor when we're interrupted by a loud beeping.

"Oh, my roast!" She runs out of the room, leaving me standing there with the painting.

As I wait for her to come back, my phone is going crazy in my pocket. So I put the painting down and finally check it. There are a bunch of texts from Jasper and Em, along with several missed calls.

Another text pops up as I'm swiping.

'GET OUT!'

My legs are frozen, and I'm still staring at my phone in disbelief when she walks back into the room. "So sorry! I totally forgot I was making a roast to take to my mom later." She looks down at my phone and I quickly hit the home key and the screen goes black. I don't know if she saw the message and her expression is unreadable.

"That's kind of you. Does your mom live nearby?" I glance around the room and try to make a mental note of the layout of the house. If it belonged to her grandfather, then why isn't her mother the one living in it? And do I have a straight line to the door if things go south?

She tries to smile, but it appears forced. "Not far. She isn't doing too well these days. It's best for her to stay in the city for now. Once I get this place up and running, I should be able to bring her here."

My phone buzzes again, and this time I jump. I hold it up in the air as a shield and excuse. "More deliveries!" It's a lie, but I want her to think someone's waiting for me.

"Of course! Thank you so much for bringing the painting. I'll send you some pictures once it's hung." She follows me to the front door and I do my best not to fumble with the knob like some weirdo. Despite the scary texts, she still seems like such a sweet woman and I don't want her to be offended.

"I love what you've done with the place," I say over my shoulder as I hurry away.

I'm about to check the latest frantic text from Em and Jasper when two completely insane things catch my eye at once.

First, the old beat-up mailbox at the end of the corner has the name Jansen painted across it in tight bubble letters. I don't even have time for my brain to catch up to the flash of memory of that name in the diary multiple times.

Because over the mailbox is a smiling brunette waving frantically at me. She's so out of place. I stutter and jerkily raise my hand to wave back before I recognize her. She walks toward me, but I no longer want to be here, so I walk toward my car...away from her.

When I get to the other side of my car, hand on the door, I feel secure enough with it between me and the house to look back up at the brunette. Her smile is gone, and she's standing in the middle of the road, unsure what to do next.

I let go of the door handle and go to her. "I'm sorry. I...I was lost in thought."

Francine, the beautiful sister of the handsome lamp guy, puts her hand over her chest and laughs. "Been there. You should see me before I've had my coffee!"

"Don't drink the stuff anymore."

"Oh...well, there's your problem right there!"

"If ever there was a time to pick up the habit again, it's now." I fight the urge to look back toward the Jansen house. She probably won't kill me with witnesses. "What—Do you live here?"

Francine points behind her. "Next street over. I like making a big square on my walk. Exactly two miles and drops me right back at my door. Are you and Abby friends?"

The name doesn't register until she nods toward the Jansen house.

"Oh! No, I was just delivering a painting. I haven't really been on this side of town much."

"Poor thing. It's so sad about her grandfather...and then her mom, too, if I'm not mistaken." She looks at me as if I have the answers.

I don't know if Abby Jansen is a murderer who was seconds away from claiming me as her next victim, but I'm still going to respect her privacy. I keep my face blank, as if I hadn't just heard that her mom isn't doing well. "Really? That is terrible."

"So!" Francine claps her hands and perks up. "Do you not get out very often at all? Or just to this side of town?"

"Um, both, I guess."

"That's a shame. How old are you? Late twenties? This should be the time of your life! You should come out with-"

"Thirty," I say, quickly, hoping to stop this freight train of another woman setting me up with her brother. As bad as Jasper dating Maura is, at least it cured Em of her sister-in-law obsession. I'm not about to let Francine start up a new one.

"Even better!" She doesn't miss a beat. "Roger said he was coming back by to get something from your cute little shop, right? Why don't I go with him and we can discuss things then?" It was not a question.

"Sure...speaking of...I better get back." I pull out my phone and type a quick, 'I'm alive' to Em. "The cats haven't learned how to use the cash register yet."

She laughs way too hard and I know I'm doomed. Her brother's cute and all, but I'm so tired of the matchmaking.

Chapter Fourteen

Sir Fluffington III

Sir Fluffington III stretches out across all three cushions on the couch. He likes to test his agility by making sure he can still reach from end to end. Also, by taking up the whole couch, he hopes to send a clear signal he is not ready to talk.

When he opens his eyes to see two pairs—green and gray—staring back at him, he knows it's no use.

"Can we not take this opportunity to rest?"

Spot stands tall, and with his best imitation of Sir Fluffington III, says, "One does not rest when they are the sole source of security for the entire perimeter."

Sassafras can't hold her laughter in. And, he must admit, it does sound like him.

"Fine." He releases his stretch and sits up. "Spot, we need eyes on the office door downstairs. Sassafras, you're on shop duty. I...will inspect the book Miss Junie was writing in. Let's see if we can get any new information before she returns. Dismissed."

Neither of them move.

"Dismissed," he says again, firmly.

Nothing.

The hairs on his back and neck raise before he even says the next word. "What?"

Sassafras uses her most innocent kitten voice on him. "Where were you last night?"

"Out."

"Where?"

"Not here."

"Where?"

Spot cuts in before he can repeat his 'not here.' "I think, sir, what she's trying to say is...anything you'd like to talk about?"

"Yes...the case."

Still, neither of his subordinates budges.

"Yeah, that's well and good but, we're worried about you. If you're in any trouble, we can help."

Not this kind.

"I'm not in any trouble. I just ran into an old friend while I was out and we spent some time catching up. That's all. Now, can we focus on our job, please?"

Sassafras nearly swoons. "What's that friend's name?"

"I'm not at liberty to say."

Spot and Sassafras exchange knowing glances and Sir Fluffington III hops down off the couch. If they will not do their jobs, then he'll just have to do all of it. But first, the book on the table. He needs to figure out why Miss Junie calls this one a notebook, but the one in the office was a diary. Humans are so confusing.

"Alright, alright," Spot says, coming up behind him. "I'll stop asking. But for the record, we think Mariel is a lovely cat. Or...whatever happened was all her fault."

Sir Fluffington III stops short of the table with the notebook and his posture tenses. "Yes, she is. And no, it wasn't."

For the first time in his life, Sir Fluffington III was ready to let someone in. To tell them what really happened that fateful day on Campbell's bridge. But when he turns to face Spot, he finds his second-in-command hissing.

He spins back around to follow the glare in Spot's eyes. As he does so, Sassafras comes bounding out of nowhere, charging toward the front door she's supposed to be guarding.

A shadowy figure is leaning against the large window, their hands cupped as he's seen humans do, trying to see inside. This figure is not one they've seen before. When it disappears, Sir Fluffington III feels a wave of relief.

Then comes the sound of someone jiggling the door handle.

Jasper

"Why aren't you eating?" Maura looks up from her giant salad and glares at Jasper's still full plate of lasagna.

He shrugs, buying himself time to come up with a plausible explanation. He knows better than to tell her the truth, which is that he can't shake this ominous feeling about Junie being in danger. That didn't go over well the last time.

"Is it not to your liking? Send it back."

"No no no!" He takes a huge bite and nearly chokes on the cheese. Still way better than the alternative. He's never sent food back in his life and can't imagine ever doing it.

Maura looks at her phone, then back at him. "I have to get back to the office soon. What are you doing later?"

"Gonna be holed up at the library for a while," he says through mouthfuls of lasagna. Now that he started eating, he realizes he was starving.

"Maybe I can swing by after the Garcia meeting, now that you've got the place to yourself." She stares at him, appraisingly. It's a loaded statement, considering they've never hung out at his apartment since he moved here. He doesn't know why, but it feels like a test of some sort. One he's about to fail.

"Let me get back to you on that. I don't know how long I'm gonna be tied up."

"At the library?" It's more an accusation than a question.

"Yeah, and the office, of course." He tries to sound as innocent as possible. "We have a lot to go over after I'm done."

"We? As in..."

Jasper sets down his fork. "Please, let's not do this. You know we're partners now. Our office is in her building. I have to go over there. It's my job." He holds her gaze as long as he can, hoping his true feelings aren't showing. He's very worried about Junie and he can't wait to get over there to prove to himself that she's alright.

As if her going radio silent at the Jansen house earlier wasn't bad enough, he's uncovered so much about the diary entries. Every one of them is another block of fear and worry stacked on top of each other. He knows he won't be able to calm down until he's at the office, going over the case. There's too much happening all at once and this case needs to be solved sooner than later.

"Seems to me," Maura says, setting her credit card on the edge of the table, "you should be more selective in your hiring process. A 'partner' you can't count on to keep herself out of trouble all the time. Seems like a liability."

"She's not in trouble," he lies. But it must have been written all over his face.

"What's she not in trouble for this time?"

"There have been a *couple* hairy situations. Nothing major. And nothing we—she—can't handle. Really, I just need a good brainstorming session to get all our theories out on the table. I think then the whole case will come together and we can solve it."

"At her house."

"At the office."

Stalemate, as usual.

"Well, if you decide to tear yourself away from 'the office,' let me know."

They sit in silence while the waitress swipes the card and leave in opposite directions. He knows he should be more concerned about the current trajectory of their relationship, but all he can think about is getting to Junie.

Something doesn't feel right.

Chapter Fifteen

JUNIPER

"What are you doing?"

Fluff winds himself between my feet again, meowing and scrubbing his face against my sandal strap.

"You've been acting so weird today."

I bend down to pet him and he slouches under my touch. I just don't know what's up with him. He demands attention, but won't let me pet him.

I look at Spot and Sass, both of whom are curled up on the dresser closest to the front door. "Do you guys know what's going on?"

Spot bares his claws, then retracts them and Sass gives me a quick meow that sounds very much like a 'no.'

I walk over to the printer and grab the next section of pages. It took way longer than it should have to isolate single frames from the video and print them out. But something told me I had to do it, so I dug the old printer out of a box in the storage closet and spent an obscene amount of time getting it working again.

As I take the pages back to the sales counter where I'm pretending to work, I thank my lucky stars for being born closer to the digital age. If I never have to print another thing—after the rest of these pages—I'll be happy.

I spread the new batch of pictures out over the counter from one end to the other. If I was strong enough, I'd move the register, too. I need more room for what's becoming a detailed timeline of whatever this is.

I still have no clue.

After situating the pages, I walk from one end of the counter to the other. My new art project starts at the beginning, with the cover of the diary and the first couple pages with logged names, all the way to the edge of the counter with the shorthand I still haven't figured out. I make another mental note to check with Em about Betty's transcription. But I can't stop now. I feel like I'm on the verge of a breakthrough.

I go back to the beginning of the counter and start again. I keep finding myself staring at the cover of this diary. Aside from being gorgeous, with the various shades of tan that bring back the memory of the leather smell, I'm mesmerized by the key. It has to go to something!

Yet again I regret my honesty, because if I hadn't given the thing to Chase right away, I'd be this much closer to figuring out what the key goes to.

That has to be the key to unlocking the whole mystery, I think, allowing myself the awful unintended pun.

I head back to the printer to grab the next batch of pages. I may have to move this operation to the floor. Or give up on the shop completely and take everything downstairs. I look up at the big clock on the wall. It's still only mid-afternoon. Waking up so early to that creepy old lady's phone call has really messed up my circadian rhythm today.

But it sure helped me get a lot done!

I take the couple of pictures back to the counter and position them precariously on the edge. Yeah, I think it's time to call it a day and take this stuff downstairs.

I'm about to move toward the door to flip the sign over when there's a loud knock. My first thought is the weird noise that's been happening a lot, but this is different. This is what I'd imagine Chase sounding like when he's knocking in an official police capacity.

I spin around to see a shadow on the other side of the door. I know I just said it wasn't that late, but it feels too late for customers. I have half a mind to flip the sign and pretend I didn't hear the knock, but then Lys's voice gives me a stern talking to and I peek through the window instead.

There's a small, frail woman on the other side. She looks older than my parents and is smiling at me so kindly; I open the door immediately.

"Oh, I'm so glad I caught you," she says in that sweet grandmotherly voice. "It looked dark in there, so I wasn't sure. I thought I missed you."

I open the door wider and wave her in. Then I look up to find that, yes, it is dark in here. Two of my bulbs are blown. I flick the switch several times, to no avail. "Hmm, I better get that fixed." I glance over to the counter where I've been working with the diary pictures, but the fluorescent light over there seems fine.

The woman's gaze scans the shop, then lands on my timeline of pictures. She walks toward them and I try to get between her and the pages so they don't get messed up, and because it's official investigative work that I really shouldn't have out in the open like this. Good thing Jasper's not here to catch an attitude.

"Oh, that's so lovely." The woman runs a finger across the picture of the diary's cover, taking her time to trace the entire key. "I had one just like this when I was a young girl." She puts the same finger to her chin. "I wonder whatever happened to it. Oh, probably lost to the hands of time. You know how that goes, right dear?" She waves the thought away, and it's clear she isn't expecting an answer.

"Sorry," I say, scooping up as many of the important pages as I can. "I'm working on a-" I stop, unable to come up with a lie fast enough.

But she doesn't seem to hear me, anyway. She's lost in her own thoughts. "They don't make them like they used to. The craftsmanship on this is wonderful. Do you have one? For sale, I mean?"

"Uh, no. That one's...gone, actually. I wish I had one. You're right about the craftsmanship. Although, I'd probably be too scared to write in it, if I had one."

"Oh, I don't know about that. Something utterly important always seems to come up, doesn't it?"

I open my mouth to answer, but nothing comes out. Then, without thinking, I ask, "Do I know you?"

The old woman smiles and puts a firm hand on my arm. "No, dear. But I am the one that called about the desk." Without letting go of my arm, she looks around the room again.

I pull my arm away and take a step back.

Jasper

Jasper throws the car in park, barely waiting for it to stop moving. He makes a split decision to go through the office door instead of running around to the front of the building. If his calculations are correct, this will buy him several much needed seconds.

As he was pulling in, he saw Junie and a figure in the shop, but over by the counter. If he can get upstairs fast enough, everything will be alright.

Or so he tells himself.

He throws the door open and barges in, slamming it behind him and stomp up the basement stairs. He needs to make as much noise as possible. Whoever's in there with Junie has to know he's coming. And hopefully think he's as big as that ax guy Junie was fawning all over.

As he reaches the top of the basement stairs, he hears Junie's voice. She sounds calm, but only on the surface. There's a current of fear underneath he knows well.

Then, as he's bursting through the beaded divider between the apartment and the shop, he freezes.

There are sheets of paper strewn everywhere on the counter. Junie's standing with her back to him, and an old woman is holding onto her arm as they walk toward the front door.

"I'm back!" He forces a light tone into his voice. He wasn't inspecting the fierce intruder to be a little old lady, and he didn't know what to do with all this adrenaline coursing through him.

From the look on the woman's face, she's terrified. He just doesn't know the cause. Did he almost give her a heart attack bursting through the apartment like that? Or did he just stop her from...what?

She's old and frail. There's no way she could have hurt Junie...right?

When the woman is on the other side of the door, Junie locks it and turns the Closed sign over.

"What was that?" Jasper asks, crossing the room quickly. He steps on a sheet of the paper as he goes to her, but doesn't care. "Are you OK?"

"Huh? Yeah, everything's fine." She says it slowly, like she's still trying to convince herself. "It-It was just weird. Maybe I'm being paranoid. All this stuff happening all at once, you know?"

"Yeah, that's exactly what I was thinking. I don't know what made me come flying over here. I just-" He doesn't know how to end the sentence, so he doesn't bother. It's clear they're both on the same page. "What's all that?" He points to the papers in her hand and all over the shop.

"It's the diary. I thought seeing it in print again would help."

"Smart. Is it working?"

"Dunno. I think it's making me crazy."

"This entire case is crazy. We need to solve it before anything happens."

Juniper

"This is so much better." I survey the vast, winding thread of print-outs on the floor. They start at the base of the stairs and spread out toward Jasper's desk. "We should move that while we're down here." I point to my desk, still in the corner.

Jasper answers with a noncommittal shrug.

"I'm not sitting in the corner of my office like it's Mrs. Durant's class all over again."

We both shudder. "You had her, too?" Jasper asks.

"Yeah, and I hated every second of it. So don't make me sit over there getting flashbacks. I'll just steal your desk."

He walks the length of our paper trail—as I try to come up with a witty joke about paper trails—and rearranges the last section so it leaves room for my desk.

"Is that everything we have?" He motions toward the stairs.

"Think so. I'll go check."

"No, you stay down here." I must make a face because he quickly adds, "with your guard cats," and nods toward my feet.

Fluff, Spot, and Sass are all lined up as if at attention, waiting for instructions. If I move an inch, they stand and reposition themselves to be on my literal heels.

"Be careful y'all. You know I'm a klutz." I nudge Sass over with my toe but gain little ground. I shrug. "Alright, but don't say I didn't warn you."

I'm about to step over Spot to work my way back to the beginning of the paper trail—I'm such a genius. I can't wait to find the perfect time to spring that one on Jasper—when the noise catches me off guard. Spot and Sass both run in different directions, and one of them is right where my foot was about to go.

I whirl around, unsure where to step, and I'm certain I feel a low vibration. By the time I do put my foot down, on top of zero cats, I'm already convincing myself it was just my equilibrium playing tricks on me. Of course, the whole house didn't move.

"Please tell me that wasn't you trying to dance," Jasper says from the bottom of the stairs. He's holding more sheets of paper against his face, as if to cover an evil grin.

"Oh, you'd know it if I was trying to dance. This whole place would be ransacked, and we'd be on the way to the hospital."

He steps down, gingerly, and shakes his head. "If you mess up our paper trail I'll-" He lets out a roaring laugh. "Ha! Paper trail. I just came up with that off the top of my head."

"Shut up!" I grumble.

I don't even want to look at him right now, so I go over to my desk to push the darn thing myself. Of course, it doesn't move, and I have to avoid eye contact for at least an hour before my pride is patched up.

After that hour, or maybe longer, I squint at the pages, unable to make out the squiggles and symbols any longer. It's gotten dark on us and I can't see a thing. Yet again, I'm reminded that I need a crystal chandelier above my desk, like the one at the Adair house.

"The house!"

"Huh?" Jasper's head pops up from his crouching position at the other end of the paper trail—my pun, not his. He's got ink smudged across his forehead, and I choose not to tell him about it.

"The Adair's house. Why have we not gone back there? Isn't that like P.I. School 101?"

"First of all, thank you for saying 'we.' Sometimes I think you have a death wish. And second, I've been meaning to go out there myself. We should-" He looks out the window pane on the office door. "-go tomorrow. And third...P.I. School 101? Really?"

I give him a raised eyebrow smirk. It's not as good as whatever paper trail pun I would've eventually come up with, but it feels sufficiently like a burn. "I was actually meaning to go by there when I dropped off the painting, but *someone* thought I was walking into a trap and scared the heck out of me."

"Well, that *someone* was your best friend. And we still don't know for sure if she was wrong. I mean, whether or not she changed the spelling, her last name is in the book."

"Diary."

Jasper groans loudly. "I really don't want to call it that."

"Sorry, I don't make the rules."

"You kinda are."

"Come on. Can we focus?" I use a page out of his playbook. "I don't think Abby's the killer." He opens his mouth, but I cut him off. "This isn't another Rusty situation. I don't know her at all. I just don't get that vibe."

"You sure got it today, though. With that old lady."

My skin crawls just thinking about her. "Yeah, something was definitely creepy about her. Or I'm creeped out in general, now. There are so many names in the book. So many people who have ended up dead. People from *here*. It's..."

"Creepy." I didn't want to say it again, but he says it for me. "Well, look at it this way. She's the only one we've come across so far who would be old enough to have kept the...journal...that long."

"Yeah. I don't know. It's hard to picture her as a cold-blooded killer." I stand up and scratch my temple. "We agree that the people in the *diary* have been murdered, right?"

"I mean, obviously. Why else would they be in a creepy notebook?"

I'm about to correct him again when his phone buzzes. We exchange glances that both say, 'It's probably Maura,' and, 'We're in trouble.'

He takes a deep breath and braces himself. Then lets it out with palpable relief. He turns the phone and I read a text from Em. 'Tell Junie to answer her phone. Lys thinks she's dead!'

My phone? I reach into my pocket as it's vibrating. There are at least ten messages and missed calls. I hurriedly push Lys's icon and call her back. "Everything alright?" I ask when she picks up on the first ring.

"Everything alright? No, everything isn't alright! You haven't answered me all day! I was worried sick!"

"Sorry, I was working and I must have been in the zone. I didn't feel it."

She takes a breath and her tone is a forced calm when she speaks again. "I'm assuming you don't mean the selling antiques zone."

"No, but don't worry. I'm safe in my basement fortress with Jasper and three guard cats. Worst that can happen to me is a nasty paper cut."

"Still, I don't like-"

"So, what did you want?" I know if I don't get her back on track, I'll be here all night getting scolded.

"Ry called earlier. He's worried about getting the big house for the trip because of the twins. I told him it would be cheaper to just stay all in one place. And if we do that, we can get tickets to the dinner theater that just opened on..."

I stop listening. Not because I don't want to talk about the family reunion, but because for the first time I'm worried, I might not be able to go. Can I leave Jasper here to deal with this all by himself? What if that old lady really is a murderer? Or if we haven't even found the killer yet and they come looking for me while he's here alone? Everything is such a mess. I don't see how we're ever going to solve this thing, and certainly not in time for my trip.

"Junie?" Lys's tone is worried and annoyed. I've been quiet for too long.

"I already told him it was fine to stay in the big house together. I want all the twin time I can get." I don't remember if that's actually what I said, but it sounds like the right answer.

Except Lys's annoyance amps up. "Is that when you stopped listening?"

"I-Sorry. My mind is all over the place. I'm trying to clear this case in time so I can-"

"You are not canceling. I don't care if you drag Jasper and an entire filing cabinet with you. This trip is happening."

That actually makes me laugh. The thought of Jasper coming along to our family reunion..." I promise I'll do my best. I don't want any of this," and by this I mostly mean Jasper, "coming near y'all and the kids."

"Y'all?" Lys repeats the word as if it tastes like ash in her mouth. "You really need to get back to civilization."

"You live in Pensacola."

"Still. You're coming. Do whatever you need to do—*safely*—to wrap this case up and get down here."

She hangs up and I frown at my phone.

"She's right, you know?" Jasper says, swiping away messages on his own phone.

"You think I sound like Miss Minnie, too?"

"What? No. Well...say, 'You didn't hear this from me, but...'"

I laugh and shake my head.

"She's right that you're not missing your family trip."

"I don't want to miss it, but-"

"And you won't." He turns his phone back around to face me.

It's a message that reads, 'Tomorrow. 10am. Come alone.'

"That's not scary at all."

His wide grin says he agrees, which makes no sense.

"Who's Carmen Harmon?"

"The woman who's about to blow this entire case wide open."

Chapter Sixteen

September 17, 2023

Sunday

Emerald

"Thank you so much for meeting me today."

Betty sits across from me, nervously fidgeting with her napkin. She's picked most of it apart, to where the Drive Brew logo is the only thing left in the center, and we've only been here a few minutes. "I've never been here. The coffee's good," she answers, picking up her mug for the first time.

"I feel bad for dragging you out of the house on a Sunday, but it's really important." I take a sip of my coffee. It's my second one today, and the last thing I need right now, but the warmth of the cup is comforting.

"No, I'm glad to meet up. And this is best done in person. I don't want my name attached to this." Betty bites her lip and I can see a tiny red dot forming. It looks like she's been doing a lot of lip biting. And it's all my fault.

"So, what did you find?"

She reaches into her purse—a large, brown suede thing that looks big enough to fit the whole table in. "This is some scary stuff, Emerald. What have you gotten yourself mixed up in?" She takes out a small spiral notebook, a size up from the one Jasper thinks makes him seem more like a cop. I notice her pale pink nail polish is as picked at as the napkin.

I reach for the notebook and she pulls it back.

"I don't know. I couldn't read the squiggles. None of us could. So we don't know what we have yet. That's where you come in." I gently lay my hand over the top of the notebook and she releases it.

"I'll tell you what. Whoever wrote that thing is sick."

She goes back to picking at the napkin.

I flip open the notebook and read some of the transcriptions.

'Walking the dog.'

'Haircut, 5 min late.'

'Interrupted by a phone call.'

In and of themselves, the notes seem harmless, but pages upon pages of them under names of people we know are now dead. Yeah, sick doesn't begin to describe it.

"Weird, right?" Betty says when I close the notebook.

"Yeah. So, what do you think?"

Betty leans in and whispers. "I think you should destroy that and the original and forget you ever saw them."

The hairs on the back of my neck agree with her, but it's too late for that. "I can't." Then I lean in to whisper with her. "My brother's a P.I. and I'm helping him. He's already in too deep. If we don't figure this out, something might happen to him. And my best friend."

"I thought your best friend ran an antique store."

"So did I," I say, and attempt a laugh to lighten the mood. "She seems to like danger more than antiques."

"Well," Betty's low whisper takes on a different tone. "It was kind of exciting. Not that I want to make a habit of it. But I can see why someone your age would get sucked in."

"Well," I reply, mimicking her tone. "If we're being honest, I'm the one who pushed her to help with these cases in the first place. I just didn't know she would get so caught up in it. And now, I feel like it's my responsibility to keep her safe."

Betty leans back and taps the cover of the notebook. "Nothing safe in there."

"What can you tell me about it? Aside from the actual writing? Did you get a sense of anything..."

"Strange? Ha!"

"Strang*er*?"

"It's definitely a stalker's diary. The dates span decades, which I'm sure you already know." She takes a swig of her coffee. There's obviously something she's not telling me.

"What?" I prod gently, then take another sip of my coffee to give her space. I feel like a real journalist, grilling a source. It's exhilarating. If this food critic gig doesn't pan out, I think I might have found my second calling.

After a moment of contemplation, she says, "There's something about the shorthand. I haven't seen anything like it in a long time. It's...impersonal."

"What do you mean?"

Betty looks past me as if lost in thought. "There are three main types of modern shorthand; Gregg, Pitman, and what we now call Speedwriting. All of which were developed in the late 19th and early 20th centuries. When I started in Secretarial College, we mostly learned

Gregg. I taught myself Pitman years later. And I've dabbled in Speed-writing, though it's not my style."

I'm completely silent when she's done explaining this, because I still have no idea where it's all going. I really hope I wasn't supposed to understand any of that.

When she looks back down at me, her smile says she didn't expect me to. "All that to say, as with normal handwriting, you pick and choose what you like best from each method and it becomes your own."

"Like a signature?"

"Yes, like that. Personally, I still use some common Gregg symbols, but I lean toward Pitman. However, over the years, I've created certain symbols that mean whole words or concepts, even."

"A short-shorthand?"

"Exactly. We all do it. Even people who aren't using shorthand will intersperse symbols into their everyday writing. An arrow here, a checkmark there. It's all very fluid and personalize, but still readable to most others."

"But..."

"But, whoever this is..." She gives the notebook another, firmer tap. "They've stayed consistent throughout, while at the same time, writing in a perfect mix of all three methods."

I scrunch my brow over the top of my coffee cup. This reminds me of something Junie said when she first opened the diary. "They did that with the normal handwriting, too. The words were all written out in perfect script, like you'd used to teach a kindergartener."

"So strange." Betty shivers, and I follow suit.

Whoever wrote this diary has spent decades covering their tracks. How are we supposed to catch them now? And what will they be willing to do to us to keep their secrets from coming out?

Juniper

Jasper and I sit in my car, idling outside of the county park. My hands are clutching the steering wheel, and they haven't moved in the ten minutes we've been sitting here.

A group of college kids are playing a casual game of soccer, but that's about it. The rest of my view is open field. Why Ms. Harmon wanted to meet here is beyond me. And beyond weird if you ask me.

But Jasper's not asking. He's messing with my AC again.

"Dude!" I smack his hand away.

"It's hot!"

"I know it is! So why did you agree to meet her *outside* in September?" He reaches for the AC again and I swat his hand away again. "It's not gonna do anything. This is as good as it gets."

"Man, next time we're taking my car."

"Em's car. And next time we're meeting in a coffee shop or an old deli like normal P.I.'s. There isn't even a park bench over here!" I point through the windshield at nothing.

"Actually, I bought it from her. And this ain't your daddy's P.I. firm."

I look at him, deadpan, and wait.

He shrugs. "I got the reference. But seriously, we don't meet in old delis or coffee shops. That's so cliché. You'd know that if you started the classes I signed you up for."

"So, you're telling me this class covers how a deli and coffee shop are cliché, but a park isn't?"

"I'm telling you to quit dragging your feet or it's gonna come back to bite us. I thought you wanted this." He reaches for my AC again but catches himself.

I don't give him a witty retort, because I don't have one. The registration confirmation has been sitting in my inbox for a week and I haven't touched it. Excuses aside, the only real reason I can think of for my lack of action is fear. What if Lys is right and I'm gonna get myself in serious danger?

Says the girl sitting at a park, waiting to meet a mysterious source.

I'm about to finally defend myself when Jasper points to a woman walking up on my side of the car. She's in her early fifties, very well-kept, and marching toward us like a woman on a mission. "There she is."

I don't know what to do. Do I open the door and get out? Go lean on the hood of my car like Starsky and Hutch? Wait for her to tell me where to go? Follow her into the empty field to my doom?

We didn't plan this far.

When I hear the door lock click and she climbs in behind me, it's the last likely scenario I would have thought of. I don't know where to look or what to do with my hands.

Jasper glares at me as if to say this, too, is covered in the class I'm procrastinating.

Ms. Harmon's hand appears between the seats. "Thank you for meeting me out here. I know it seems paranoid, but it's necessary, believe me."

Jasper comes right out and asks, "Is Carmen Harmon your real name?"

She nods, clearly used to getting this reaction.

With my free hand, I smack him, then with the other, I shake her hand. With a name like Juniper, I'd never judge someone else for theirs.

"Thank you for meeting with us. I can't imagine how this must look, us contacting you out of the blue."

She pulls her hand away and reaches into a briefcase that I'm just now noticing she has at her side. I'm so good at investigating. "Not really out of the blue. I expected something big to happen now that the old woman's gone."

"You mean, Mrs. Adair?"

"Yes. She was the last piece of the puzzle. I've been trying for years to get my story out there, but it kept getting shot down. Maybe you'll have better luck." She pulls out a thick manilla folder, bound by large rubber bands, with tons of papers shoved inside. Multi-colored tabs stick out from every direction.

"Wow," Jasper and I say together.

"You don't know the half of it. This is my travel copy." Ms. Harmon unwraps the rubber bands and starts leafing through the papers. "I have stuff going back decades, long before things started happening in this town."

As she rifles through her notes, I catch glimpses of old newspaper articles printed and taped or glued to sheets of paper. Pictures of several people, some of whom I recognize as now deceased names from the diary. Other blank squares with writing all around them, where I presume a picture was once, but is now gone. Names are written everywhere, some are crossed out, more still are written again and crossed out again.

What I don't see is any shorthand.

A part of me I hadn't realized was on alert finally relaxed.

"What got you started looking into the family?" At first, I think I've said this because it's exactly what I'm thinking, but then Ms. Harmon turns toward Jasper and I realize it was his voice I heard.

"A friend."

Jasper and I both cut eyes at each other, then back at her.

"Can I see it?" Ms. Harmon asks, both and neither of us in particular.

I don't make a move, but Jasper reaches into the glove-box to show her some pictures we printed out. The cover is on top, followed by the list of names and a couple pages of shorthand. "The cops have the actual journal now, but this is some of the information we could collect."

I butt in to correct him. "We believe it's a diary of decades of stalking at the very least, but most likely something way worse."

"Amazing."

I give her another minute to leaf through the pages. "Did you see anything like it in your investigation?"

"No, not at all. I haven't seen shorthand in...forever?" She holds one page closer to her face. "Fascinating."

"Can you read it?"

"It's..." She brings it closer still. "I don't know. I can catch bits and pieces, enough to give me a bad feeling. But, no, I don't think I'd be a good source for translating this."

Jasper waves her comment away. "It's fine. We have someone working on that. But whatever you can tell us would be helpful."

"It's mostly just random stuff." She runs her finger down the page. "I can only catch a few words here and there, like 'dog' and 'car' and 'ice cream.' I think they were stalking someone, for sure."

"Does that align with your own investigation?" Jasper sounds so professional right now. I'm reluctantly glad he's here because I wouldn't have the presence of mind to ask the right questions. I need to get my butt in gear and start the class.

This makes her give Jasper back the printouts and pull a smaller journal from her briefcase. "I tried to condense everything here after you called. Everything's so jumbled. But from what I can gather, this all stemmed from a failed proposal." She's still flipping through pages in her notebook, but looks up when I gasp.

"Are you telling me someone went around killing a bunch of people because they got dumped?"

Jasper huffs. "Oldest motive in the book."

"No, I don't think it's that simple." Ms. Harmon points to a particular line in her notebook. "The failed engagement set off the chain of events that led to this diary and string of crimes. But he was already active long before then."

"He?"

Ms. Harmon looks up at me. "Yes, he. Or more accurately, 'they.'"

Jasper leans back.

I put my hand over my mouth. "I don't like this."

"What are you saying?" Jasper asks when he gets his voice back.

Something Rebecca said comes back to me. "Mrs. Adair's maiden name is Hess."

"Yes. E. Hess *is* Mrs. Elizabeth Adair."

I can't believe I forgot about that! I remember thinking about E. Hess and Mrs. Adair...when was that? What made me-

Fanzella!

I was this close to figuring it all out when he accosted me at the Greasy Spoon!

"Wait a minute..." Jasper's voice is low, like he's still putting the pieces together. "So, he stalked her before they got married? Romantic," he says with disgust.

"And it didn't stop there."

"Of course it didn't."

Ms. Harmon taps her notebook, her finger resting on a particular name. She takes a weary breath before saying, "A. Bauer is who Elizabeth Hess intended to marry, before Ed Sr. got his claws into her."

I swipe through the notes app on my phone. "A. Bauer; Aston Bauer died in 1991 of heart failure at the age of thirty-seven."

Ms. Harmon purses her lips together and nods. There's something unreadable on her face, but Jasper interrupts my thoughts before I can decipher it.

"Back to the 'they' part. Are you saying this couple killed her ex? For what? And then a whole bunch of people after that? And haven't gotten caught in forty years?"

"Do we even know they were killed? Heart failure..." I trail off. Heart failure at thirty-seven doesn't feel very natural. I scribble down a note to check into that.

Jasper must be following the same line of thought because he says, "So far, they all look like natural causes. The ones we've found, at least. But that's one heck of a coincidence. A lot of names in one place who happen to be dead."

"Yeah, but..." I close my eyes, trying to make the swirling thoughts coalesce. "Nothing we've seen so far proves that the person who wrote the diary is the killer. It could be a journalist. This is shorthand, after all."

Ms. Harmon bites her lip. I can tell she's been wanting to say something ever since Jasper cut her off. I give her a pleading look and she says, in a whisper, "Aston Bauer was my granduncle and he did not die of natural causes, whatever that book says. A book, might I add, that you got from where?"

I glance at Jasper, who nods.

"It fell out of an old desk I got from the Adair house."

"Oh, I bet they're scrambling to get it back."

"Who?"

"The kids. Her grandchildren. There are three of them, absolute menaces to society, all of them. Have you not heard about them yet?"

I rack my brain, trying to remember what I know about the Adairs, but it's not much at all. I feel so inadequate sitting here with Jasper and Ava, my inexperience evident. All I know is what Ms. Minnie told me. "They had three kids and the oldest might not belong to Ed..." It doesn't feel good spreading that last part, but it could be important.

"Yes, that's the rumor. I never followed that line of inquiry, but it's a poorly kept secret in town, especially with our parents. Are you from here?"

Jasper and I nod and I say, "Yes. We both moved away, but we came back recently." She smiles in a way I don't like. "Not like that," I add quickly.

Jasper agrees, waving a hand between us. "Strictly business."

Her smile doesn't fade. "Well, you may have missed it, but the Adairs have been fodder for the quilting club for decades."

"I'm sure that's how I heard about it...not from quilting, but from a prominent member." I can't help the small chuckle that follows, thinking of Ms. Minnie and her friends airing dirty laundry while literally creating more.

I expect her to laugh along, or at least give me a polite smile. Instead, I'm met with an icy stare.

Way to go, Junie. Did you forget how she's connected to this whole thing?

"I-I'm sorry. I wasn't trying to—I know it's a-"

"What?" She snaps to attention. "Oh, no, you're fine. I never knew him. I was just thinking." She takes out her phone and starts typing. "I didn't include this in my initial investigation, but it's always bothered me."

She turns the phone around for us to see that Mrs. Adair's first husband died in 2014 when he crashed an experimental plane during a flight lesson.

"Wait wait wait." I hold my hands up. "I thought you said your uncle was-"

"That's part of the confusion all these years. The *first* Mrs. Adair was Elizabeth Hess. She was betrothed to my granduncle, Aston Bauer. Her son Ed married Elizabeth Morris-Bugg, whose first husband, Michael Bugg, died in the plane crash."

A shiver passes through me and not at hearing the word 'bug' twice. "He married someone with his mom's name?"

She nods. "And it gets even better. Their oldest, whether he's Ed's by blood or not, is Edward Adair IV, and their daughter is also Elizabeth Adair."

"I'm so confused."

"Me, too," Jasper says for the first time in a while. He's mostly sat here watching us talk with his mouth hanging open. "We need to get back to the office and figure this out. Carmen, thank you so much. You've been a tremendous help."

Ms. Harmon—I'm still not comfortable calling someone her age by her first name—shakes Jasper's hand, then pulls yet another manilla folder out of her briefcase. "I wasn't sure about you two at first, but I think this is the right thing." She gives me the folder as she shakes my hand. "This is a copy of everything I have in my folder. I hope you get farther with it than I did."

She gathers the rest of her things and leaves us alone, staring at each other.

Jasper moves first, taking the folder from me and smiling. "Glad I didn't insist on driving," he says, pointing toward the steering wheel. It's a dig at me because I did insist on driving when we got in my car. That seems so long ago.

I don't start driving yet. I need to get my bearings. So I text Em, 'Come to the office. We have big news!'

Within seconds, her reply says, 'Already here. So do I!'

Chapter Seventeen

I DON'T DRIVE MY little Honda like a race car the way Jasper would, which is why I demanded to drive in the first place, but I sure push the poor thing to its limit. I don't want to look at my speedometer to see exactly how fast—plausible deniability—though the surprise on Em's face when we pull up is enough of a sign.

We wait until we're inside and down the stairs before starting. The cats follow us and each picks a person. Sass demands that I pick her up. Spot jumps in Jasper's lap and curls up. And Fluff settles for Em, though makes enough of a show of letting her scratch his chin that she wouldn't know the difference.

"So," I say, pushing Jasper out of his seat and apologizing to Spot for the interruption. Then I take the seat and settle in with Sass, then look at Em. "What did you find out?"

When Jasper huffs, Spot jumps down out of his arms and walks to my desk, clearly being the only one of the two who got my hint. Jasper follows and starts pushing the desk across the room toward us. It's too heavy, by far, but I let him struggle with it. I've been asking him to help me move it for days now.

Em takes a small notebook out of her bag and hands it to me. "I met Betty at the coffee shop and-"

I spin around to give Jasper an 'I told you so' look and catch him giving me one right back, but I'm sure for a completely different reason.

Em continues, ignoring our antics. "It gave her the creeps as much as it did us. That's for sure. She said it was a mix of different shorthand, but also perfectly written, kinda like what we saw with the normal writing. She didn't say the word 'code', but that's the only thing I can think of. Someone went through a lot of trouble to keep this secret."

"For sure." Sass pats at the notebook as I'm trying to read it. Seeing the pages I've come so accustomed to staring at, now with actual words under the symbols, is surreal. I wonder if this is what an archaeologist feels like when they decipher hieroglyphs or an ancient tablet. Though, to be fair, this isn't ancient. "Or is it?"

Em's eyebrows raise and she makes a noise.

"Oh, I was thinking out loud. This is really old. I mean, if someone started this diary in the 1920s, they'd be a hundred by now."

Jasper grunts. "Over." He stands from trying to push my desk and comes to us to read over my shoulder. "Assuming they were old enough to write, and learn shorthand, in 1925, they'd be well over a hundred now, if they're still alive."

"Mrs. Adair?" I ask. "She had to be really old for Ms. Minnie to call her-"

"Can't be her. She's in it."

Em gasps. "What?"

"Yeah." I nod. "Remember Becky said her maiden name was Hess? Well, she's the E. Hess at the beginning of the book. I think it all started with her, or at least the recorded part." I tap the notebook and scan a couple more pages, skimming.

"Grocery shopping. Dinner with L. Out of town. Garbage."

Em puts her hand out like she doesn't want to hear any more of it.

Jasper leans over my shoulder more to read silently with me. Sass finally gives up and jumps down.

We read another few pages of more mundane entries that span more than a decade, before Jasper says, "It has to be Mr. Adair. The first one…Or I guess he's a junior? I don't know. But it has to be him, right? Since he was stalking her."

"But he's been gone," I say, pulling up my scribbled notes. "He died in '94."

"Who else could it be? Mrs. Adair just died, right? In order for you to get the—are we still gonna call it a diary if he wrote it?"

I jerk back in my seat, surprised. "What? Of course. You think only girls can have diaries, Jasper Earl Irons?"

"No?" He stretches the word out like he doesn't believe it.

Em answers for me in her big sister voice. "It's a diary. Deal with it."

I hand the notebook back to Em and go outside to the recycling and grab a cardboard box. I give it to Jasper and say, "Cut it and tape it." I point to the wall beside the map. Then I get a Sharpie out of Jasper's desk and add 'whiteboard' to my mental supply list.

After he's finished taping the flattened cardboard to the wall, I run through theories.

"OK, we start in the 1920s with someone following E. Hess, who later becomes Mrs. Adair. I'm gonna call her number one to keep track." I write all that on the board.

Then I draw a table with three columns and write, 'Name, Symbol, and CoD,' on the top. "Alright, let's run through what we know about every person."

Jasper reads out the information, and I start the list. "E. Hess. No symbol. Unknown cause of death. Lawson Hewitt, unfilled stop sign, heart attack. Melanie Vincent, wavy symbol, disappeared. Not sure if they're dead or not."

"I'll put an asterisk beside it."

Em interrupts before Jasper starts the next line. "Doesn't that wavy line mean 'sort of' or an estimate?"

Jasper and I both stare at her.

"What? I remember *some* things from school. And that was a fun little squiggle to write in math class. So I remember it." She shrugs as if that makes perfect sense.

"Could be," I say, and move over to the side of the cardboard to draw each symbol I remember from the diary; a check mark, an X, the stop sign, both filled and unfilled, the long curve that looks like the bottom half of a circle, and the wavy line. Besides that one, I write Em's explanation. "OK, what else?"

"Aston Bauer, filled stop sign, heart failure." Jasper says the words slowly, and I write them just as slowly. Then he adds, "Poor Carmen."

"What?" Em asks.

"Aston Bauer was Carmen Harmon's granduncle," I tell her. "That's how she got involved in all this. I don't know if it's why she became a journalist, but I'm sure it had something to do with it."

"That's the reporter you met with?"

We nod.

"Wow, that's terrible."

"Yeah, puts it into perspective," I say. I sigh heavily and tell Jasper to keep going.

"Nikolus Jansen, unfilled stop sign, pneumonia. That's your painting lady's grandfather."

"Abby," I say, not liking how he described her. "If her grandfather's in the diary, she's a victim, too. And her poor mother's failing health. Wait!"

"What?"

"Should we be checking this against what Ms. Harmon said in her files? Before we go this far?"

Jasper shakes his head. "I want to get our theories down, then cross reference them with hers. We still don't know exactly how she's involved. Her family member is in here, remember?"

"So you don't trust her?"

"I do...to a point. I'm going to verify what she has in her folder before it gets added to ours."

"You trusted her enough to tell her about the diary and how I got it, but you-"

"I didn't tell her. You did."

"No, the way she asked that question, she already knew the answer. And I looked at you for-" I can't say the word permission, so I skip it and keep going. "-before telling her it fell out of the desk."

We both fall silent.

Did she already know about the desk and the diary before we contacted her? "How did you find her?" I ask him.

"Her article..." He closes his mouth, then opens it. "I was gonna say I found her name on an article, but I actually found a reference to her article on a genealogy site. Not the article itself."

I have no idea what that means, but I write that, too, off to the side. "OK, next?"

"Scarlett Stafford, X, still alive."

"Hmm," I say, hand hovering over the cardboard.

"What?"

"How do we know that's the right S. Stafford? If they're alive, an X feels counterintuitive, right?"

"It could mean they stopped following her."

Em asks, "Wouldn't that be a stop sign?"

"Well, there's only one S. Stafford in the whole town, and she's still alive."

"Alright." I write it down and add, 'stopped following' beside the X on the other side of the cardboard.

Em squints at all my notes. "Someone's getting a whiteboard for Christmas."

"Someone's not waiting that long."

"Next is Beatrice Abbott, wave, unknown."

As I'm writing this, I glance over at my notes on what each symbol could mean, and I don't like what I find. The last person with a wave disappeared.

"Michael Bugg, plane crash."

I write the name but stop. "What symbol."

"He's not in here, but I think he should go on the board. He's related to all this, somehow."

I cross him out and write his name off to the side. "That's part of her research, remember? We'll add it when we verify." I throw his words back at him.

He shrugs as if that's fine. "Samson Walters, X, unknown but most likely old age. He was ninety-two. Mario Chavez, long curve, car accident."

I get a flashback of our last case. "Single person?"

"No, and it doesn't appear to be his fault."

I write it down.

We continue like this until Jasper keeps coughing and clearing his throat, and my hand aches. I've resorted to writing tiny at the bottom of the cardboard to keep from writing on the wall. The only thing that stops us is the mystery noise.

I know it's not all in my head now, because Em and Jasper freeze. "You're right," Em says, "I can't tell where it's coming from."

"I know. It's driving me nuts!"

The cats scatter, also going mad from not being able to find the source.

Jasper stretches. "I think it's a sign."

"Of what?"

"Of me needing a break. Let's get you another box and start working on suspects and theories."

I smile despite the thought of my hand breaking from all the writing. I have to admit, this is the most fun I've had in a while. "Yay! You know, Mr. Bartlett on the corner just bought a giant TV for their lobby."

Jasper groans but heads out the door to snag me a nice box.

An hour later, I've fed the cats, got us some snacks, and am standing in front of an entire wall of cardboard waiting to be written on.

"What if we have it all wrong?" Em is standing over my desk, which is in its right place finally, but has become the snack table. It's a paltry offering on such short notice; half a bag of chips, old trail mix, and a lone cucumber I bought a few days ago when I was feeling ambitious. No wonder she can't decide.

"About what?" Jasper asks, wiping his brow and pulling up his seat. Spot doesn't give him time to recover before hopping back in his lap.

"What if it's just someone like Ava keeping notes?" She points across to the open manilla folder on Jasper's desk. "She stalked several people during her investigation."

Jasper leafs through the folder quickly. "Did any of them end up dead?"

Em shrugs. "Not my job to find out."

"None of this is your job."

"Alright, you two," I say, uncapping my marker. "Theory one; journalist." I write that on the left side of the new cardboard. Something about the squeak and smell of a Sharpie that makes me want to solve all the crimes. "What else?"

"I'm just saying," Em continues, "If her grand-whatever is one of the supposed victims..."

"You didn't see her, Em. There's no way she's involved in this other than trying to solve it like us."

"Maybe she had help."

Jasper chews on the side of his lip.

"What?" I ask.

"The journal didn't have to start back in the '30s." Ah, he was reluctant because he didn't want to agree with his sister.

"Correct. The *diary* could be a new tool for...whoever—journalist or killer. A way of compiling all their stalking and possibly murdering notes from..." I can't bring myself to say 'a century,' as I write the clue on the cardboard. "Are we looking at more than one person?"

"I think we have to," Jasper says quickly. "A father-son team?"

Em tosses a chip at him. "Or mother-daughter."

"But of course," he says, picking the chip off his shirt and eating it.

"So..." I write that on the board as well. "Do we think we have an actual killer, or a journalist, or a stalker?"

Jasper taps on his phone a bit. "I've been trying to get answers on some of these natural causes of death. And the disappearances. And now a possible plane crash?"

"Too many variables. No pattern."

"Exactly. Unless that *is* the pattern."

"Or we're dealing with more than one person," I say, bringing us back where we started.

"What if Carmen went after the Adair family because of what happened to her granduncle? And helping us is just to throw us off the scent?"

"She said he didn't really die of heart failure. So, what? He died of a broken heart and she—and another person—killed all these people?" I tap the marker on the first list we made, which includes Aston Bauer.

Jasper makes a face that says he doesn't believe it either.

I step to the right and point at the top of the cardboard where I've written 'Suspects.' "Let's move over here. Maybe this will help." Reluctantly, I put Carmen Harmon's name up top, though I don't think she'll stay. Then I add a line for the whole Adair family, because it's too convoluted to figure out right now. "Who else?"

Jasper sneaks a chip to Spot. "The old lady."

"Which one? And stop that. If you give one a chip, I have to give all of them a chip and I'm not getting that whole mess started."

Em reaches into the bag and pulls out a broken chip for Sass. She sniffs it and scrunches her nose. Then she tries to feed it to Fluff who looks at her like she's crazy.

Jasper smirks and gives Spot another. "The one who called you then showed up here. Which one did you think I meant?"

"Mrs. Adair number one."

"Put them both up. They're both old enough...I think."

"But one's dead now."

"Has there been another murder since she died?"

"I don't think so." I write Mrs. Adair and the old lady on the cardboard. "She could have just been interested in the desk. I don't think she actually did anything bad. I could have just been weirded out because of everything else going on."

Em picks up a floppy cucumber slice and puts it back down. "True. Calling very early in the morning isn't bad. Nana used to do it all the time. But showing up here right after, and grabbing you?"

"I really don't know." I put an asterisk by her name, as well. That makes me feel a little better about her being up there. "So that really only leaves the Adair family...killing themselves?"

Jasper nearly jumps up. "What about the ones who disappeared? What better way to commit the perfect murder than to not exist?"

I like that! I check the other side of the board and write down the names of the people who are unaccounted for. My good feeling disappears when I have to write Trixie's grandmother down. This whole thing is such a convoluted mess still. I don't see how Chase ever solves anything!

"Still doesn't explain how the stalking started in the '30s. A couple of those people didn't disappear until way later. They could be behind Mrs. Adair's death, but not the whole diary."

Em walks up to me and I hide the marker behind my back. She laughs and says, "Don't worry. I wouldn't dream of it." Then she pulls another marker from behind *her* back and starts writing on my cardboard! If it was anyone else, that would be dangerous, but from her, it's funny.

Down the far left side of all the cardboard, she lists all the Adairs, from the first set of Ed and Elizabeth on down to the three grand-children. "Do we know for sure how all of them died? Or how many have?"

I try to remember what Ms. Minnie says about them, but I don't remember any cause of death. If it was anything scandalous, surely she would have been more than happy to tell me. I consider asking again, but I don't want to draw suspicion, or become the subject of her next conversation.

My silence prompts her to point at Jasper. "Figure that out. What about the first Mrs. Adair? She's the one who just died in the house, right? Do we know anything about that?"

I shake my head. "Rebecca said it was natural causes. And if she had anything to do with this diary, she had to be old enough for that to be the logical conclusion."

Em shakes her head back at me. "Yeah, but she'd also be too old to kill any of the recent people. Or to stalk them, for that matter."

"Ms. Minnie said she hadn't seen her for a while. She actually didn't know whatever happened to her, and you know how rare that is for Ms. Minnie. So either she became a recluse or she got sick."

"Or she went into hiding," Jasper adds.

Of all the things we just said, Em writes that one down.

I'm not sure I believe that, though. "If anything, it started with her husband. The original Mr. Ed." I wait for them to catch the joke but they don't.

"Yeah," Em carries on, "He was watching her before they got married. The creep. Even so, he's been dead for a while. And so have the next Mr. and Mrs. Ed and Elizabeth Adair." Em's shoulders come up like she's seen a spider.

It is rather unorthodox and I don't know what to make of it yet. Marrying someone with your mom's name, when you already have your dad's name. Or you can't help who you love. I'm surely a testament to that. Mark's face pops into my head and I mirror Em's disgusted shiver.

"So," Jasper says, standing up and putting Spot on top of his desk. "It's settled."

Em and I look at each other, then at him. I know nothing's settled for me. My head is spinning.

When we don't answer, he keeps going. "We're looking for more than one person, probably someone in the periphery of this...book, who stands to gain something by people around the Adair family going missing, at the least."

Him calling the diary a book is a step in the right direction, so I don't correct him. As for the rest of his statement, I can see the logic, just not how he got there. I'm sure if I say that out loud, I'll get another lecture about taking the P.I. course, so I say nothing.

It's obvious he's ready to leave, so I cap my marker and Em does the same. I don't know how I feel about today's conclusions, but maybe some sleep—and a peek at the course—will do me some good. Until then, Jasper seems to have a handle on theories.

"What's our case?" I ask, utterly confused.

"All of it," Jasper says, as if that's the most natural conclusion.

"This is too big to solve. It's been going on for a century. A century!" I repeat.

Em circles the first Mrs. Adair's name. "This is your case. The one that started it all. And the one whose death started all of this." She uses the marker to draw an air circle around all of us.

Jasper yawns in response and it forces me to do the same. "Alright," I say, tossing the marker at him. "Let's sleep on it and regroup tomorrow."

Em tosses her marker, too, harder than I did. "Great! And in the meantime, no going to meet strangers alone. No casing abandoned houses. No...anything that will lead to your untimely death."

I put an arm around her shoulder to show both of them out the office door. "Don't worry. The farthest I'm going tonight is my comfy bed."

"No," Jasper says kind of loudly.

"No, what? I can't go to bed?"

"No, don't touch that door. It's secure. We leave through the shop so I can make sure that's also secure." He doesn't wait for a response before heading upstairs.

"What's that about?" I ask Em as we follow him.

She leans in and whispers, "Chase gave him a strong talking to after you went gallivanting around town all by yourself."

I roll my eyes. "I'm not some damsel in distress who needs to be saved by the big, strong men in my life!"

"But it makes them feel better to think they're protecting you. I let Eddie open the pickle jar yesterday. You should have seen him light up."

"You're so bad." I let her go first up the stairs and get out of arm's reach before asking, "You think his real last name is Adair?"

"Ew! Don't even joke about that!"

When we get up to the shop, Jasper's standing there with a piece of paper in his hand and a scowl on his face.

"What's that?" I ask, taking it from him.

He doesn't have time to answer before Em snatches it and nearly squeals with delight. "Looks like someone has an admirer."

I snatch it back and read it.

Dear Juniper,

Roger and I came by to see you, but the shop was closed. Hope everything's OK. Would love to get together again soon under better circumstances.

Hearts,

Frannie & Roger

Em swoons and bats her eyes. "Juniper and Roger, sitting in a-"
I push her out the door and lock it.

Chapter Eighteen

SEPTEMBER 19, 2023

Tuesday

Two days have passed since our marathon mystery session in the office, and I still feel no closer to solving this thing. Jasper's practically radio silent and Em's cagey about what she'll talk about with me. I'm getting major flashbacks of when they were both keeping big secrets, but this time I'm sure it's just that we're all overwhelmed.

I know I expected the meeting to answer all my questions, but instead I'm full of new ones, and these are even harder. Like, could the original Mrs. Adair really marry her stalker? Did she know? Did she take part in stalking and possibly worse later? Could Ava, or Abby, or Trixie have anything to do with the diary? Or Mrs. Adair's death?

Jasper, before he started ignoring me, found that the second Mrs. Adair died during a routine surgery. So she's the first, and only, name crossed off the long list downstairs.

Now, as I endlessly rearrange things on the shelves to make room for the dish set Lys won't let me keep, I'm more focused on the diary itself. Or more specifically, the key on the cover. We didn't discuss it at all in our meeting and it's been nagging at me ever since. It has to go to something, right? Something important. Why else would it be on a murder diary?

Hoping to find out what I was missing, I finally started the P.I. course. I wish I'd done it so much sooner. Don't tell Jasper. The first section was all about investigative resources, things I never knew existed. I signed up for every one of them. I tried researching the diary itself, first. None of my pictures show the manufacturer or copyright dates, not even a signature or initials in the leather.

Then I took the image of the key itself and tried to work on that. Reverse image search found a lot of matches, but nothing concrete. But I had a place to start. Every near miss was a late 19th century wooden trunk. Naturally, all I could think of was treasure chests!

Now, all I can think of is tracking down the treasure chest that goes to this key, and what it all means for the case. This whole thing has been a whirlwind and now adding a treasure chest into the mix is mind blowing.

I can't take it anymore!

I put the cherub figurine that I'd been moving back on the shelf I had gotten it from and head to the door. I don't know where I'm going, but I know out there is closer to the answer than in here.

"Can you guys please behave while I'm gone?" I ask Fluff and Spot. I have no idea where Sass ran to after I stopped her from chasing Peep back under the refrigerator. I thought we were past this, but I guess she's still learning.

"Where are you going?"

I spin around to see Chase in full uniform, staring down at me.

"Nowhere."

Fluff makes a noise that could be mistaken for a sneeze if it didn't feel like a condemnation.

"Mmhmm," Chase says as if he agrees.

"What's up?" I walk toward my apartment as if that's where I was headed the whole time. I even hold the beaded curtain, so it doesn't hit him. "You look so official in uniform. Am I under arrest again?"

He doesn't crack a smile. "You weren't under arrest then. It's not my fault you keep getting your prints all over evidence."

"Mmhmm," I parrot back to him.

"Speaking of..." He lets me sit down before starting.

"Uh oh." My mind reels about what I've touched lately and how close I just was to going out and touching more stuff I shouldn't. Who will feed the cats if I go to prison?

"Where is your case file?"

"My what?"

He scans my apartment, then asks again. "Your file on the journal? Where is it? Downstairs?"

He moves toward the trapdoor, but I jump up. "Why are you interested in my file? You have the diary in your possession...don't you?"

"Yes, but that's not what I'm interested in."

"Good, then give it back," I tease.

"Juniper." He uses my full name, and it wipes the grin off my face. "I need to see what information you've gathered on your own."

"Fine." I lead him down the stairs to the office. I almost tell him he has perfect timing and can help me set up the dry erase boards I just bought, but something tells me that's a bad idea.

When I grab the file from under the roll top of my desk, I gather the courage to ask, "Can I see what's on the pages I'm missing?"

He takes the file from me and feels the weight of it. "Seems like you have plenty."

"I know there's a lot of stuff in the middle of the diary that would really help us solve this-"

"Us?"

"Are we really playing that game again? Jasper's legit. I'm taking the class-"

Chase lets out a breath and starts flipping through the folder. He comes to a page that interests him and takes it out.

"Careful. It took forever to get those in order!"

Ignoring me, he holds the page up and points to a name. "What do you know about this man?"

I squint, although I see Aston Bauer's name perfectly well. It's a clear stalling tactic I'm sure won't work on Chase, especially since it was in the first module of my P.I. class. Rookie stuff.

"Junie, this is important." At least he's back to using my real name.

"I know he was supposed to marry the first Elizabeth Adair until Ed stole her. And then he died."

"Have you been in contact with anyone regarding Mr. Bauer recently?"

I press my lips together.

"I just got off the phone with Jasper." He lets that hang in the air.

"You had a question about our case, and you went to Em's baby brother first?" I take the file back from him and shove it in the rolltop. I don't slam it, because I don't want to hurt the desk, but I sure would love to. "Then I'm sure you got whatever it is you think you need from him."

Is this why Jasper isn't answering? Does he know he's gonna catch an earful when I get ahold of him?

Chase pulls out his phone and types something. Then he asks, "Do you know this woman?"

At first, I don't look. I'm trying to get control of my expression before seeing Carmen's face. But when I see the actual image staring back at me, I can't control anything.

It's the old woman who called in the middle of the night, then showed up here unannounced asking about the desk. She has a stern look on her face, like she's angry at whoever's taking the picture.

"Did she do it?" I ask.

"She's dead."

"She's what!?" I clutch my chest, then my hand goes to my mouth. I can't believe I just said she was the killer. I look over Chase's shoulder at her name on the Suspect list and feel a pang of guilt. I want to go cross her out right now, but Chase is still talking.

"Been trying to contact her granddaughter for notification, but she's not returning my calls. I was hoping-"

"What does this have to do with Mr. Bauer?"

"The victim, Loretta Bauer, was his sister. She and her grand-daughter have made quite a few enemies in town under the guise of investigating his death all those years ago." He swipes his phone again, but this time I'm prepared for what I'm about to see.

Carmen Harmon's professional headshot smiles back at me.

"What happened?"

"We're not sure, yet. Looks natural, but...considering her proximity to the case and-"

"So, there is a case?" I almost regret the glee I hear in my voice. But I can't help it. I've been going in circles about whether this was all some fantasy in my head, mass hysteria between me, Em, and Jasper. Now Chase has confirmed there really is a case.

He looks around as if we're not the only two people in the office—minus all three cats who have suddenly appeared very interested in what we're saying. "Mrs. Adair was found during a welfare check after her son said he hadn't heard from her in a while. She...had been gone for some time."

"Welfare check? So, she'd been alone in that house? For how long? How old was she? Wouldn't she have...I don't know, *someone* there with her?" My list of questions has just grown exponentially. They're coming faster than I can think of them.

"She was a fiercely private person."

"I bet she was!" That comes out before I can hold it in. I'm equal parts ashamed for thinking ill of the dead, and worried Chase will ask what I mean by that. Honestly, I wouldn't know where to begin.

I finally gather the strength to walk over to the cardboard and cross out Ms. Bauer's 'name.' I can't believe just two days ago I was fine with calling her a creepy old lady. My finger brushes against Carmen's name, which I had also not wanted to write up there in the first place. I want to cross her out while I'm at it, but can I? What does this new clue mean?

Surely she didn't kill her own grandmother? She was trying so hard to prove Aston Bauer didn't die of heart failure. Why would she- "Are you investigating Carmen for this?"

"Right now, I'm investigating everyone."

My eyebrows go up.

"Almost everyone. Please don't give me any reason to suspect you and your...partner."

I bark out a laugh. "No better way to drum up business for a P.I. firm, huh?"

He takes a step closer. "Can't you see how dangerous this is now? You just spoke with this woman a few days ago and now she's gone. Her granddaughter, who you also had recent contact with, is missing. This is too dangerous!"

"Missing?"

"Why else would she not respond?"

A weight settles over me. Chase is right. Too many people close to me have disappeared, or worse. "When did you talk to Jasper?"

Sir Fluffington III

"This is not a drill!" Sir Fluffington III gathers his subordinates in the corner. Sassafras had been on probation after the Peep incident that morning, but matters have changed. He needs all paws on deck.

Miss Junie and Mr. Chase were still talking by the wall she had been writing on the other day. Strange, when he got mud all over the wall that one time, it was a big deal, but she can write on it and everything's fine.

Focus!

Spot has taken up a position a few steps behind him and Sassafras. It's his job to listen for any new revelations while Sir Fluffington III comes up with a plan.

"Now that there's been a development of this magnitude, we must-"

"Mag-ni-tude?" Sassafras asks, slowly.

"Big," he answers, quickly. "Now that someone Miss Junie knows has died, and another is missing, we need to be on high alert. There's no doubt in my mind that she's going to slip out of the house as soon as Mr. Chase leaves. We have to be ready."

Spot meows from his post. "They're talking about Mr. Jasper and Miss Emerald. She sounds worried."

"Can you tell what they're saying?"

"Miss Junie told Mr. Chase she was going to go check on Miss Emerald and he said he would do it, and for her to stay put."

"Well, we know that's not gonna happen. As soon as he leaves, we're on duty. Spot! You follow Miss Junie wherever she goes. Sassafras, you stay close to Mr. Chase. If anything has happened to Miss Emerald, you get right back here. Miss Junie will need snuggles."

Sir Fluffington III shudders at the thought, both of something happening to Miss Emerald, and that he says the word 'snuggles' out loud.

Sassafras nods solemnly. "What are you gonna do?"

"I need to figure out who is behind all this and put a stop to it." He breaks the huddle, but Spot puts a paw out.

"Do you recognize any of the names they said? From your time on the streets?"

"Me or the kid?"

"Either one. You might know the older people. Did you recognize the woman when she came to the shop?

"No, she didn't smell familiar. I smelled her again when Miss Junie came home the other day, but now we can assume that was her scent on the missing woman. How about you, Sassafras? Do you know any of the other people from your time outside?"

She twitches her nose and looks up at the wall as if trying to read Miss Junie's writing. "I-I wouldn't know anyone by name. The only people I remember by name are Mr. G and his family, because they were nice. Everyone else was by sight. The lady at the bus stop who always dropped muffin crumbs. The man who would sometimes set his coffee down and forget about it. The mean lady with the pointy shoes who stepped on my tail too many times for it to be an accident."

"That's terrible, kid." Sir Fluffington III moves closer and wraps his tail around her.

"Thanks. I'm alright now. You and Miss Junie have kept me safe."

Sir Fluffington III's heart melts, then breaks, because what he's asking of her now is anything but safe.

Before he can change his mind, and her assignment, Spot hisses at them. "It's time!"

Miss Junie walks Mr. Chase to the door and tells him to text her the moment he gets to Miss Emerald's house. Then she closes the door behind him, locks it, and runs upstairs.

They all follow her and none are surprised when she waits behind the window for Mr. Chase's car to leave before grabbing her keys and running out the door.

Lucky for them, she's so busy watching the red lights on the back of his car that she doesn't see them dart off in the other direction.

Chapter Nineteen

JUNIPER

"Hey!" A female voice calls from the side of the building. "You running off again? We already missed you once!"

My hand is in the air, key almost at the lock, when I hear her. It takes a second to place the voice. My mind already on leaving, and on what Chase will find at Em's house. I *know* she's fine. But it wouldn't hurt to have him check on her. And it was a great ploy to get him out of the house so I could leave. But now...

I turn to see Francine in a nice, long coat. I'm about to comment that she must be burning up in that thing when Roger comes out from behind her. He's dressed more appropriately for the weather, board shorts and a faded blue shirt. Though it doesn't look right on him, specifically. With his broad shoulders and a couple hundred pounds over me, he isn't what I would call the surfer type.

"Oh, hey! I was..." I trail off, not sure what I was about to do, now that I think about it. Was I really going to run off to an abandoned house to snoop around? Something tells me the answer is yes, but also that I should keep that fact to myself.

"You're a busy bee," Francine says, giving me a tight side hug. "Ever since Roger told me about your shop, I've been dying to get in here and see what you've got going on." She gives her brother's arm a big squeeze and, if I'm not mistaken, pulls him closer to me as she does so.

"Well," I say, scooching away and opening the door, "not sure what you're in the market for, but I have a lot of really cool items. You said this was for your mom, right?"

"Right," Roger agrees, and holds the door for me and his sister.

"So, what do you think she'd like?" I wave my hand at all the items at the front of the shop. Lys rearranged everything when she was here, putting the fancy stuff by the window and the 'impulse' stuff on the corners. To me, it looks wrong, no rhyme or reason. But it seems to work. I keep having to refill the corner sections.

But now, when I'm trying to steer a customer toward an item, I don't know where to point. So, I gesture to everything.

Roger scratches his chin, surveying the shop. "You've changed it up."

"Yeah, I can't decide what I want to do with the place yet. It's still new." He chuckles, and I take a second to catch my joke. "Yep, new old stuff!"

Francine joins in with an overly polite laugh. "That's funny! You didn't tell me how funny she is, Roger."

I step toward my sales counter, not for the panic button, but maybe. If she doesn't stop pushing us together, I'll have Chase and the entire police force here in minutes!

He seems to ignore her, or he's as done with the matchmaking as I am. He turns more toward me and makes a show of looking around at our feet. "I see your guard cats are off duty."

I follow his gaze around the empty, quiet room. "Hmm, guess so." Wonder where they went.

"Are they investigating that noise? Did you ever figure out what it was?"

I shake my head.

Then, he tells Francine, "That's what interrupted us last time. Some weird stuff going on in this house."

"All the better," she says. "The only thing Mother would like more than a gorgeous antique item is one with an equally amazing story behind it."

"Well, you're in the right place! I think I told your brother before, but I know the story about everything in here."

"Really? What about this?" She picks up the cute little cherub I'd been rearranging earlier. Good thing I didn't move it, I suppose.

"Aww, that was from a yard sale in Annapolis, MI. The family had a set of three, but this was the only one left. I felt bad for it and brought it home with me. I tried looking for its siblings a few times over the years, but to no avail."

"Aww," she mimics, and pulls the cherub to her chest.

Roger touches the lamp he'd been looking at his first time in here. "How about this one?"

"That's a funny story, actually. The original owner of this building, Mrs. Horwitz, ran a store out of here, as well. But she could never bear to part with this lamp, so she kept it hidden for years in the apartment. I was going to keep it in there, also, but she said it was time. She'd kept it long enough that it's now an antique, so what better way to start off my new store than with her old lamp?"

"Wow, so you and this town go way back. You must know a lot about the people, too. It seems like a tight-knit community." He walks closer, but stops at a quill and ink set. I'm preparing myself to tell the story of how I came to own that, when he asks, "Does your family still live here?"

"No, just me. I moved back home at the same time as they were all deciding to leave it. Go figure." I shrug it off, but it hits me how true that statement really is. I hadn't thought of it that way. At least I have Em to come home, too.

I hope!

I shake off the bad thoughts. "So, what else would you like to know?" I reach for another item off the shelf, expecting them to ask for another provenance.

Instead, Francine inches closer still. So close that Roger has no choice but to brush up against my arm. "What's the craziest item you've gotten your hands on?"

Of course, my mind is reeling at the recent drama my antiques have brought on, but that's not the sort of thing you discuss with potential customers. No monkey paws sold at this shop!

"I don't know," I say with a half shrug. I'm careful not to move the shoulder nearest to Roger, for fear of touching him or sending the wrong message. "Most people think it's crazy for someone my age to collect any of these things, and even crazier when you find out I've done it my whole life. Imagine a five-year-old girl freaking out over a creepy old doll covered in dust in the back of a thrift store." I nod and point to my chest, then to the far corner of the shop where Felicity sits, untouched.

Francine darts down the aisle toward her. "Now that's what I'm talking about!"

My heart skips. I don't think I can give up Felicity. That's why she's way in the back, where nobody ever goes. Lys promised me she'd be safe there.

A firm hand takes mine. "Don't worry. Mother isn't into dolls. She does love..." He pauses, exaggeratedly looking around the room and bracing himself. I take too many seconds to realize he's joking about the noise that interrupted us the last time he tried telling me what his mom would want.

I duck slightly, to let him know I finally get it.

"Mother's always loved personal things, like old books and fancy pens and...things people hold near and dear. You might say she collects lives."

I don't know how to respond to that, and luckily, I don't have to. Francine groans behind me and says, "Please excuse Roger. He's so melodramatic sometimes. What he means is, she collected personal stories. Autobiographies. Diaries. Photo albums. That sort of thing."

It's at this exact moment I realize Roger is still holding my hand. I pull it away and use it to pick up the quill and ink set. "Well, then. You're in luck. This was rescued from a 19th century freighter before it sank off the coast. It's also one of the last of its line, since the inventor-"

There I go again. *Do not tell your customers the owner of an item died holding it!* That has to be rule number two or higher.

"It's perfect," he says, gently taking the items. I drop my hand the second he has them, to not risk brushing knuckles.

I hurry to the counter and ring them up. Francine makes a joke about free delivery, but I don't give her the appropriate amount of polite laughter. They've overstayed their welcome and made it abundantly clear they didn't come here for antiques.

And I'm not for sale.

Yet again, I wait at my door, watching a car leave before I can. I check my phone. Still nothing from Chase. So I send him a quick, 'Dude' to get his attention.

I'm about to give up on my plan to go treasure hunting—a thought I never expected to have unironically in my adult life—and go check on Em myself. Then I see Ms. Minnie waving at me and get an idea.

"Hi, Ms. Minnie! How are the flowers today?" I lock my door and head over to meet her on her side of the road.

"Very nice. I love the switch over to fall plants. Such lovely colors and the smells are divine. Always remind me of living on the farm as a little girl. I see your business is booming, too."

"It is, actually. Thank you."

"And the *other* business?" She gives me a wink.

"That one, too. It's exciting! That's kinda what I wanted to talk to you about."

Her thin gray eyebrows rise. "I didn't do it. I was tending to my flowers the whole time." Her denial sounds too sincere. I almost don't catch the curve of her lip. It's the twinkle in her eye that gives her away.

"You just let me be the judge of that," I say, playing along. "But for now, what else do you remember about the Adair family?"

"Oh, yes, I heard about poor Beth being in that house all alone. I thought for sure one of her other kids came and got her after Ed Jr. passed. Such a shame." She puts her hand over her mouth, the smile and twinkle gone.

"Do you remember the other kids' names?" I pull out my phone, still no response from Chase, and open my notes app.

"Gloria and Michael. Good kids, as far as I know. Gloria took in Ed's little ones after Liz's surgery. I guess I just assumed they all went to live with her."

"So, Ed died before Liz?"

"Yes, a couple of years. But I hadn't seen Beth since long before that. I figured it was her ailing health and all. And after Gloria took the kids, I guess I just thought the house was empty all this time." She reaches over to preen one of her sunflowers and I see her hand is shaking.

I save my note and swipe away from the app. "Thank you. I'm sorry to bring all this up."

"No, it's fine, dear. I hope Chase and his men—or you and Jasper—can find out what really happened. That sweet woman deserves closure."

"The whole town does." What else am I going to say? She may have been stalking and killing everyone in her path for nearly a century?

"You heading out to catch the babies?"

I take a moment to remember that's what she calls the cats. I turn around in a full circle, looking for them. "Did they get out? I was wondering what happened."

"Yeah, the first time you were leaving, after Chase, they took off down that way." She points toward downtown. "Except that one." Now I follow her finger to Spot, sitting on the hood of my car.

"What in the world?" I give Ms. Minnie a hug and cross back over to my side of the street. "Get down from there!"

He merely meows at me and licks his paw.

"You can't go with me. It's too dangerous. Why don't you go find Fluff or Sass?"

Spot hops down and weaves himself between my ankles.

I pick him up and I'm about to take him inside when my phone buzzes in my pocket. It's a thumbs up emoji from Chase.

Spot meows and nuzzles up to me. I give him a big squeeze, more relieved than I thought I'd be. I knew she was fine, but part of me needed that reassurance. I look at Spot, then open the car door and plop him down on the seat.

"OK, but don't tell the others. I can't get in the habit of taking you everywhere."

Especially when 'everywhere' includes the scene of a possible murder.

Sir Fluffington III

Sir Fluffington III waits for the cop car to pull out of the driveway. He recognizes the man behind the wheel as the one Ms. Emerald brought over to the apartment. He knows he can trust him, but not how much. Better to be safe and stay back.

The man served his purpose already by leading Sir Fluffington III to the location. He knew if he followed one of the cop cars, he'd have a good shot at ending up at the victim's house.

Now, with the coast clear, he can take his time conducting his own investigation. He had been close enough to overhear some of Mr. Eddie's conversations, so he knows where to start. He slinks across the yard, careful to step inside the footprints that are already pressing down the grass. Not that he'd be heavy enough to make a dent...with all the training he's been doing with his subordinates.

He really must start referring to them by their names. After these past few months, they deserve it.

Actually, he could do with a little help from Sassafras now. The only open window he spied was the rounded one above the door. It's only one pane, probably too small for Mr. Eddie to notice, and possibly too small for even his more lithe frame.

Sir Fluffington III thinks thinning thoughts and hops on top of the shrub to the right of the door. From there it's a quick pounce to the awning and in he squeezes. As he lands, he congratulates himself for still being at the top of his game. Not a hair out of place.

The house is dark, but that doesn't slow him down. He walks the perimeter of the living room, careful not to step near the yellow number cards on the floor or up on the table. He's watched Mr. Chase work enough crime scenes to know those are important. Why else would they be yellow?

He sniffs the carpet, then follows the trail to the back of the house. Yes, it's stronger in here. Once you've smelled the bitterness of fear, you never forget it. The bedroom door is closed and wrapped with yellow tape, but he doesn't need to go all the way in to know, this is where it happened.

There are scuff marks on the floor and a small handprint on the wall. Whatever made the victim come to the room, she was scared. And she wasn't alone.

"Bad kitty!" The voice startles Sir Fluffington III enough to slow his reaction time. His feet move but the rest of him doesn't. It's a fraction of a second, but all the time the man in white needs to reach down and grab him.

Chapter Twenty

JUNIPER

I should text Jasper to tell him where I'm going. If all my time investigating cases—and module one of the P.I. course—has taught me anything, it's that you need to wait for backup. What the class hasn't covered yet, is what to do when your partner rats you out to the cops. How much could we have learned on our own by now if Jasper hadn't told Chase about the old lady—Ms. Bauer coming to the shop?

Not worth the risk. Besides, I have my trusty guard cat here. I reach over and pet Spot as I turn toward the Adair house. He stretches to his fullest height, looking ready for anything. Maybe I went about this all wrong, trusting humans to have my back when I already have my kitties.

The street is quiet as I pull closer, nothing like the last time I was here. I didn't appreciate the gravity of the situation then. I was in the house, almost touching the yellow caution tape, and all I could think about was *things*. Sure, it was a bustling estate sale with people and chatter all around me. But with all that stripped away, it's a scary, dark, empty house.

And I'm turning off my car to go inside.

I feel a little guilty, choosing to search for the treasure chest I know goes to a key I don't even have, instead of trying to find Carmen Harmon. I don't believe she's the killer, so her going missing might be for her own good. Or she's not missing at all and Chase just hasn't gotten ahold of her. Or I'm just rationalizing it because I really want to find that chest!

Either way, I roll down the window and tell Spot to stay put. Neither of us believe he'll do it, but at least I said it.

Maybe, if I survive this, I'll swing by Abby's to see how the painting's doing. She had to know the Adair family at least a little, if her grandfather lived over here. Maybe she has information I can't get on my own because Chase has the diary. I've almost fully crossed her off my list, but it couldn't hurt to check. Well, it could—a lot—but I'm already on this side of town and already doing stupid things today.

I'm already at the door before I bother to think about how I'm going to get in. But that becomes a moot point, because the door is open. If I weren't breaking and entering—minus the breaking—I'd tell Chase he needs to be more careful about securing crime scenes. Instead, I grab a decorative broom off the porch and push it farther. Technically, I didn't open it, the broom did.

I go straight for the previously taped up door, which is now closed, but unsealed. I brace myself for what I might find. Who knows if the original Mrs. Adair was involved in the events of the diary? I have a good inkling that she was. But this is still the room where someone died, good or bad, treasure chest or no.

I wipe the sweat off my palms and enter the room. It's as expected, very hundred-year-old-woman-lives-here. Lived. Honestly, I hope she wasn't a murderer because everything in this room is just my style. The four post bed, Narnia style wardrobe, and glass wash basin on the nightstand are absolutely flashes of my future.

Too bad Becky didn't let me loose in here, because I would have bought everything. It's heaven as far as the eye can see. But what my eye doesn't see is a treasure chest full of murder secrets. Yet.

"If I were a secret murder box, where would I hide?"

I look at the Narnia wardrobe, hoping that's not it. But rule number one of private eyeing...follow every clue, even the ones you don't like. That's gotta be up there, right?

The handle sticks, and it takes a few good jiggles to break free. With it comes a picture frame, toppling onto my head from above, then falling to the floor. I hadn't even noticed it was up there, which I'm sure was also at the top of the P.I. rules. Notice your surroundings before they hit you over the head.

I bend down and pick it up, taking notice of the three smiling children, two boys and a girl in the middle. There's something mesmerizing about them, and not just the vintage clothing that's coming back in style. They look so innocent, the older boy with his arm around the girl's shoulder and the younger boy with his reaching up to give her bunny ears.

I smile at how some things stand the test of time.

Still, there's something else about them. I'm assuming this is one of the Eds and his siblings. From the clothing and sepia tone, I'm guessing it's the most recent owner of the house. That would make sense, considering this is the original Mrs. Adair's room. These would be her children. So why can't I put the picture down?

I have half a mind to pull the photo out of the frame and stuff it in my pocket to study later. The other half, though, has morals, and I put it back on top of the wardrobe. Then I give it a little push to make sure it doesn't fall on me again as I finish snooping.

There's no wooden chest in here, and boringly, nothing more than normal items for someone who lived a century. Clothing that ranges from Kentucky Derby hats to bloomers to a very smart pant suit. Nothing to suggest either way if I'm standing in the room of a murder or one of their victims.

Em's voice plays in my head again, as it's done on repeat since our meeting. 'Could be both.' Em's right. She could be the killer and now a victim. All the more reason to stop dilly dallying and find that treasure chest. It has to hold all the answers.

I still take my time leaving the room. I don't know where to look next. I was sure my treasure hunt would start and end here. Get in and get out before anyone knows you're-

There's a loud creak on the other side of the door and I freeze, telling myself it must be Spot, but also knowing he wouldn't weigh enough to set off even the most finicky floorboard. When the next thing I hear is whispers, I'm certain it's not Spot.

I spin around, freaking out, and assessing the situation in a full panic. At least I'm on the bottom floor this time, I think as I approach the window. Surely, I could jump out and get to my car before anyone catches me.

My car! What if they saw my car? And Spot!

Worry for my cat overtakes my self-preservation and I sling open the door, ready to rush whoever's on the other side and save Spot.

I crash right into Francine, who stumbles backward and knocks Roger over. His flashlight drops to the floor and barely misses her toes.

"What are you two doing here?"

"We could ask you the same thing!"

"Me? I'm-I, uh?" I can't get my tongue to work. Francine and Roger stare at me, as if I'm the only one here where we don't belong. "Actually, I asked first." I puff my chest with as much authority as I can muster.

Roger makes a noise and Francine covers for him. "What are we doing? In our house?"

"Your what? I-I'm so sorry!" I scramble to get out of the house-their house! Roger steps in front of me.

There's a hiss from the door and we all turn to see Spot, hackles up and teeth bared. The sight of him causes Roger to make that noise again, but this time the tone is more amused.

Francine puts her hand out between us. "I'm sure there's a plausible explanation."

I nod. "Of course! I was..." *looking for a murder box that matches a key I found on a murder diary.* "The door was open."

Francine smacks Roger on the arm. "You left the door open! See. Juniper, here, was just checking on the place. Very neighborly of you," she says in my direction.

Again, I just nod. Spot meows. My phone buzzes.

When I pull it out of my pocket, we all look down to see who it is.

I answer slowly. The last thing I need is for them to yell that I'm breaking into their house. "Chase? Hi, what's up?"

"Emerald's alive," he says.

I already know this from his previous thumbs up text, which means he wants something. What I want is to hurry up and get off the phone.

To get out of here! I use the call as an excuse to move closer to the door. "Thank you. I guess I should get used to her ghosting me a little, now that she's got a boyfriend and all. I'll let you get back to-"

"Waldo's?"

"You're at Waldo's?"

"On the way. You craving some nuggets?" He knows I hate it when he calls them that.

"Always! I'll meet you there!" I hold up the phone toward them. "I gotta go. Again, I'm so sorry for the mix-up." I bend down and scoop up Spot, who lets out one last warning hiss. On the way to the car, I whisper to him, "Hush. We're the ones trespassing."

Francine's voice is right behind me. "I'm starving! Are you starving, Roger?" She doesn't wait for either of us to answer. She opens the front passenger door and shoves Roger in, right beside me, of course.

The last thing I want is to be forcefully match made, but I also just technically broke into their house, so I owe her this. Still, I let Spot loose in the car and he takes his seat, whether or not Roger's in it. We spend the next twenty minutes in silence, aside from Spot's grumbling. I'm more than a little satisfied at how Roger's white-knuckling the door handle.

Chase is already there when we pull up. Normally, I'd be irritated at him, always wanting to sit outside, but this time I'm glad. With Spot and our two uninvited guests, I need the freedom of movement. He watches me, then Francine and Roger get out of the car, and his expression darkens. When he finally sees Spot, he's unreadable.

Still, he gets up from the table and comes to greet us. "Roger, Francine, nice to see you again. Under better circumstances, this time." To me, he says, motioning to Spot. "Will he behave himself around my fish?"

"I dunno. Better be safe and not order it."

"Too late!" His smile, which had faltered at the change of plans, was back with a vengeance.

He leads us all to the table and Waldo's there to deliver the herring and tenders. "Hey, what'll you have to drink?" Then he sees Spot. "Which one is this?"

I turn Spot around to show of the orange blob on his shoulder, his namesake. "Spot!"

"Maybe Chase'll share-"

"No!" Chase answers before he's even done."

"Waters, please," Francine says at almost the same time.

We all sit, and I try to settle Spot in my lap. He's having none of it, but it's Roger he's interested in, not Chase's herring. If that's not a big red flag against whatever Francine thinks she's doing, I don't know what is.

"Sheriff Adler," Francine says, sweetly. "I didn't know you and Juniper were an item.'

I'm glad I haven't touched my chicken tenders yet because I'd have choked on them. "We're not!"

"Ouch," Chase says. "But Junie's right. We've been friends since childhood."

"Aww, that's so cute. Roger and I kinda kept to ourselves as kids, so we never got the hometown experience."

That makes me perk up. If the Adair house is theirs, that means they're Adairs. And they should have grown up here with us. But I've never seen them. "Were you homeschooled?"

"You could say that." Francine puts her hand on her brother's upper arm. "Roger here didn't need much schooling. Boy genius over here. But I needed all the help I could get."

I raise my brow, more at her than the object of her affection. I'm not taking that bait. I also would never say anything remotely that glowing about my brother or sister. Then again, I'm not trying to set either of them up with someone.

Waldo arrives with their waters and a thin slice of herring for Spot. From the sounds he's making on my lap, it's much appreciated. "Have you two decided?"

"Oh, I haven't even looked." Francine makes a show of flipping the menu over.

Roger finally speaks for himself, saying, "We'll have burger platters. No mustard on hers. Ranch for my fries."

"Perfect," Francine says, handing her menu to Waldo.

I side eye both of them. She's trying to set me up with a guy who orders for women. No, thank you.

Chase catches me and clears his throat. "So, how long are you in town for?" He says it gingerly, like it's a sore subject.

Francine and Roger both respond, tripping over each other. "We've almost gotten what-"

"...Arrangements have been made..."

"-Last requests."

Chase nods in response. "That's to be expected. As soon as the investigation is complete, we can turn over..." He trails off, and lucky for all of us, Waldo comes back at that exact moment with Francine and Roger's burgers.

As if the situation at the house wasn't awkward enough, the silent lunch—aside from Spot voicing his appreciation for his slice of fish—is the least comfortable thing I've been through in my life.

And do I still have to drive them back to the house they caught me breaking into?

'Where are you?' Jasper's text pops up as soon as I'm back on the road after dropping Francine and Roger off. Yes, I had to take them back to the house they busted me breaking into. No, I didn't get anywhere on the murder treasure chest. No, I didn't swing by and check on Abby or the painting. And no, I didn't fall for any of Francine's not so subtle hints that her brother is single.

'On my way!'

Spot settles into his passenger seat, glad to have it all to himself again.

'Hurry up!'

'Why?'

'Don't text and drive. Just get here!'

I press the pedal enough to follow Jasper's orders to hurry, but barely. I have precious cargo with me, after all. I reach over and pet Spot as we make the final turn. "Alright, don't tell anyone where we went or that you got fish. I'll never hear the end of it."

He purrs in response. Somehow, I feel like he understood me and he's pretending to be asleep.

Jasper's waiting at the office door when I pull in, with a strange look on his face. And Fluff in his arms.

"What's all this?" I ask, taking my cat from him.

"Someone was at the old lady's house."

At first, I think he's talking about me, but then I catch his gaze trained on Fluff. Oh, the other old lady. "How did you get him? Were you there?"

"No, Grady was closing up and forgot his glasses. When he went back for them, he found your naughty cat instead. When you weren't here, he called Em, who called me. The words 'his mother's son' might have been mentioned." He reaches over to give Fluff a scratch behind the ear.

Fluff and I both stiffen. "I don't know what you're talking about. My cats are very well behaved."

Spot chooses that exact moment to jump out of the car, startling Fluff—and Jasper—and chaos ensues. It takes several seconds of claws and hisses for Fluff to realize who the intruding cat is. Which is several seconds longer than it takes for Jasper's hand to suffer the consequences.

Fluff dismounts from my arms and chases Spot through the backyard, while I shove Jasper inside. "Glad you're here, anyway. I've been thinking."

"Oh, no." He lets me lead him to the supply closet and grab the first aid kit.

I dab a cloth with alcohol. "We need to get a clear picture of what we're dealing with here. It's still too big, too nebulous."

"Nebulous? Ow!" He jerks his hand away.

I yank it back. "I barely touched you. Hold still."

"What's not clear about the picture? The Adairs killed a bunch of people and then someone killed them, or at least one of them."

"Do we know for sure they were killed? I just...Francine-"

"You talked to Francine again? And, I'm guessing, her brother?"

I choose not to discuss exactly how I talked to them. "Yes, and it got me thinking." He makes another noise and I want to rub him with the alcohol swab again. "There are so many people who went missing or are confirmed dead, but we don't know how, not for sure. And I think the only way we're gonna figure this out is to find the pattern. In the deaths, the symbols, the dates they were being followed, maybe. I don't know. But we need more information than what we have."

He doesn't let me put a Band-Aid over the scratch. Instead, he pulls out his phone and brings up his pictures. "Here," he says, swiping through them. A bunch of people I half recognize start scrolling past me. "Heart failure. Car accident. Definitely poison made to look like natural causes. Convenient hiking accident. The list goes on."

"Hmm."

"Hmm, is right. There's no way this is a coincidence."

"No, you're right."

"And your new boyfriend is-"

"Eww!"

"Think about it, Junie. What happened all the other times you stumbled onto a murder?"

I shrug, not wanting to admit what he's about to tell me, anyway. But he doesn't answer for me. He makes me say it. "Someone connected to the crime sniffs around me and my shop."

"Exactly."

He's right. I've felt it, somewhere deep down, ever since running into them at the house. Because if it was really their property, why would they need a flashlight?

Chapter Twenty-One

Sir Fluffington III

Sir Fluffington III tires from chasing Spot around the yard and herds him back into the house. All three of the cats convene on Miss Junie's bed, ready to give their reports. He's dying to know where Spot went and how he ended up in the car, but he knows his information is more pressing.

"The old woman who came here looking for the desk is dead. And she was not alone when it happened. I got interrupted, but I'm sure I've smelled the person who was with her before. I need time to think and I'll have a report. What about you?" He turns to Sassafras.

"Mr. Chase went to check on Miss Emerald, but I couldn't get over there fast enough. By the time I got to the corner, he was already on his way back. So I followed him...to a restaurant...where I saw something very interesting-"

"I got fish!" Spot doesn't wait for her to finish. "We went to this old house and Miss Junie snooped around a bit. Then I heard other voices and went to go check on her. And I found her in the front room with that man and woman who keep knocking on the door. And I almost had to fight him, but then Mr. Chase called and we went to an actual restaurant and I got a fish!" He stops to take a breath.

Sir Fluffington III paces at the foot of the bed. "So, you saw the man and woman at a house? And then Miss Junie took you to a restaurant?"

"She took all of us. They went, too. It was awkward. He sat in my seat."

Sassafras hasn't moved off the fish yet. "Did you bring us any?"

He looks sheepish for a moment, then shakes his head. "Sorry. Maybe next time."

Sir Fluffington III stands between them. "There won't be a next time. We need to focus. What's our next move?"

Sassafras flicks her ears at Spot. "Find out what they're talking about right now and follow that lead."

"They're talking about all the people around town who keep turning up dead. I don't know what it all means, but I do know, I recognize the person who was at the latest victim's house. I just can't place his scent."

Chapter Twenty-Two

Wednesday

Juniper

Today has been busy. I've had no time to myself, no time to think, or make headway on the case. As I usher the last customer out the door and begin to flip the Closed sign, I'm glad Lys isn't here to catch me complaining. Which reminds me, I never replied to her last text about the menu for our trip. Who makes a full menu for a weeklong vacation? My sister.

There's a knock, and I let go of the sign, unflipped.

Ok, one last customer, for Lys.

When I plaster on my smile and open the door, Carmen appears from out of nowhere. I grab her arm and pull her in.

"Carmen! Are you alright? Chase was looking for you. Your poor grandmother. I'm so sorry. Why didn't you tell-" I get all of those words out before noticing the look on her face.

She steps aside as Roger shoves his way in, his hand firmly on her shoulder. This is the first time I've seen him without his sister since his first visit. The surrounding air is much colder without her incessant talking. How did I not notice that before?

"Hi!" That comes out way too bubbly for whatever's about to go down. I lower my tone and try again. "Back for more? How did your mom like the-"

Carmen's brow furrows and Roger huffs.

His mom is—was... Oh, I'm in trouble.

Sensing the change in atmosphere, the cats come running. Fluff sniffs the air and charges at Roger. Spot and Sass follow quickly behind and before I know it, all three cats are on him.

But something tells me not to stop them.

Carmen and I exchange worried looks and in the confusion, Roger's grip loosens. We retreat toward the sales counter, but a yell stops us.

"I wouldn't do that if I were you." I slowly turn to see Roger holding Fluff, whose teeth are sunk into his forearm.

"Put him down."

He shrugs. "You might want to tell him to put me down first."

"I'm sure he has his reasons." I'm still inching toward the sales counter, to the panic button. I've never tested it out and I don't know if it's going to scream at us when I push it, but I have to do something.

Carmen stands firm as I pass her. "Your own mother?"

"How dare you insinuate I would touch a hair on that poor woman's head?" Roger moves closer, causing Spot and Sass to take swipes at his legs.

"Why?" At first, I don't recognize my voice. Or that I said the word out loud until it turns his attention on me. I freeze. "Were you tired of waiting for your inheritance?" I feign innocence, though I'm sure by now he knows I have the diary. I showed my hand when I went to the house, especially when they busted me in her bedroom, of all places.

"Money? You think I care about money?"

I shrug. "All murders boil down to one of three reasons," I say, reciting what I read in module three of the P.I. course. "Love, money, or revenge."

He chuckles and shakes his head, then moves closer still. Fluff scratches and hissing, all while holding firm to his forearm. "You're forgetting one."

"Compulsion." It's not in the class, at least not that I've seen so far, but it's the only thing that would explain the diary. Who would go through all that trouble if they weren't under some spell? "But...you're not...Who..."

My phone buzzes on the counter, loudly vibrating and scaring all of us. This causes Fluff to let go of Roger's arm, but Roger doesn't let go of him. Not at first. As they're struggling, I reach for my phone to call Chase.

Then I see the text that caused all this mess. It's from Chase. 'Hey, did you sell a fancy old typewriter recently? There's one at this crime scene and it looks like one of yours'

I send back a quick emoji of a police siren and a string of exclamation marks.

When I look back up, Fluff is on the ground, blood is dripping from Roger's arm, and he has Carmen by the hair with the other hand.

"Where is it?" Roger demands.

"I don't know what you're-"

He shakes Carmen and she lets out a cry. "Don't play with me. I don't have time for this!"

"Don't give it to him!" Carmen's cry turns into a growl. "He's not worthy."

Not worthy?

It takes a second to hit me. I know what she's doing. "Yeah, you're right. I don't think he's worthy. If he was, surely they would have brought him into the fold. Or maybe they tried and he was so careless he let the desk get sold out from under him, with their murder diary taped to it. Rookie mistake, if you ask me."

"No one's asking you! And the desk wasn't for sale. It was in the basement! When we found out what that woman did, who she sold it to...She should've been next. Maybe she still will be. After I clean up this mess." He shoves Carmen in my direction, still not letting go of her hair.

"You expect me to believe they trusted you with the diary? With their secrets? You think you're gonna carry on some family legacy? Stalking and murdering women? You can't even *talk* to them without your sister-"

"You leave her out of this! The diary is mine! I earned it! You heard her. I'm a natural."

"A natural? How are you gonna clean up this mess? Make this not point straight back to you?" I gesture toward the rest of the shop, landing back on him and Carmen.

She snorts. "He's not. He's too weak and impulsive. He's destroyed the whole family legacy in one fell swoop."

"Really? You don't think I have a lot of practice making things look like accidents? I've been at this a long time, ladies." He pushes Carmen into me without letting her go and I bang my hip on the counter. It hurts, but I'm glad to have finally reached it. Now all I need to do is distract him enough to hit the button.

"Your blood is dripping on my floor."

"So," he says, shaking even more of it off. "You think I need a Band-Aid for my little boo boo? Like your boyfriend?"

That catches me off guard, but I recover quickly. He's been watching the place. Hoping to catch me with the diary. I shake my head. "Actually, I meant that you've contaminated the crime scene with your own blood. So, not much chance of this looking like an accident. Especially not with Carmen here. The cops have been looking for her ever since-"

"Ever since you killed my grandmother!" She punctuates the last word with an elbow in his rib.

Roger buckles over, enough for Carmen to get away again. I direct her with my eyes to run behind the counter and mimic pressing the panic button. She's fumbling for it as Roger collects himself, and when he stands up, his face is red with rage.

I rush to the end of the counter so he can't catch her. "The cops are onto you! This won't do you any good."

"Onto me? You mean the cop who literally ate lunch with us yesterday?" He reaches into his waistband, and I charge at him.

We tumble to the ground, me and all three cats on top of him. He roars like an animal and pushes us off. I go flying. He's so much stronger than he looks. Must be all that ax throwing.

I cringe as soon as I think it. "Self-preservation, Jupiter," I whisper to myself as I stand up.

Jupiter?

Juniper. I rub my head, wondering how hard I hit it.

"Yes! The cop who just had lunch with you and your *sister.*" I don't think I believe that anymore. "So if I go missing or end up dead now, who's the last person I was with?" I raise my eyebrows at him.

"Your *business partner,*" he says, will full finger quotes. "Or her." He points to Carmen, then reaches into his waistband again. This time I'm too far away to stop him.

I can't get to Carmen in time, either. The only thing I'm good for is covering my cats. I dive on top of them and brace myself.

Instead, I hear a laugh. I lift my head enough to see him standing over me with a tiny cop notepad in his hand. What is it with men in this town and tiny cop notepads?

"You're making this too easy." He bends down to pick me up and a loud, shrill noise breaks my eardrums.

At first, I think it's the noise we've been hearing and that something really wrong finally happened with it. Then I hear Carmen yelling, "Help! Help!" over the top of the noise.

The panic button. At least it works! Not enough to make him run screaming, though.

"How am I making this too easy?" I ask, stalling.

Roger ignores me and runs behind the counter. He smashes the panic button several times, trying and failing to stop the noise. So he grabs Carmen again and shoves her toward me.

Then he takes a couple steps and pauses in front of a late 19th century chest of drawers. "Well, I was going to make it look like an accident." He nods toward the cats, who are all squirming to get loose from me. "Maybe you got clumsy, tripped over one of your cats, hit your head on this beautiful dresser with the dangerous claw feet."

Now I'm the one red with rage. How dare he include my cats in his evil plan!" I'm still kneeling, but I lunge for him, anyway. I clip his knees and land on top of him again.

"Now I see why you have to resort to killing old ladies. And why they didn't trust you with the family business!" His brows shoot up. "Yeah, I know you're an Adair, and that you're so bad at killing. You didn't get the diary."

I snatch the tiny cop notepad out of his hand. Just as I thought, it's full of shorthand notations and the name at the top of this page is mine.

"It's a ledger, not a *diary*." He nearly spits the word out.

I sing back, "Diary," like a jingle. "But seriously, I've been wondering. What do all the shapes mean? Like, is a stop sign really murder? What's the X?"

He struggles to get loose, but now Carmen's standing over him with my broom handle raised. "X means we're sure they'll never be found, which is what I've decided will be next to your names." He smirks and looks up at Carmen. "You almost did that one for me, but you had to come back, didn't you?"

I freeze. For the briefest moment, I expect her to turn the broom on me and do a triple cross spy reveal. But she only tightens her grip. "My grandmother was onto your family long before I came along. You aren't the only one who's taking over the family business. Well," she shrugs, "I guess *I'm* the only one now. Since you'll be locked up."

"Does Francine know you're like this?" I still can't figure how she plays in all this. Is she really his sister? Was there a fourth secret kid nobody knew about? "Is she your mother?"

"Ha! The age difference, huh? Yeah, no. I'm the baby of the family. Francine was happy when I came along and took the heat off her. She didn't have the stomach for it. But no, I'm just a mid-life surprise."

"Not a good one."

Another laugh. "It's gonna be a shame to have to kill you." He reaches for the broom handle in Carmen's hand and forces it to swing in my direction.

I leap back and grab the nearest thing I can get my hand on, and whack him upside the head. I hear a crack and quickly inspect the vase for damage.

Carmen pulls a roll of masking tape out of nowhere and we are wrapping his wrists just as Chase runs in.

"Wha-" He can't get the word out and closes his mouth, staring at the three of us. "Ms. Harmon! I told you to stay out of sight."

She gives Roger's binding a good yank. "He was coming for her. I had to act."

Now I'm the one staring between them with my mouth open. "You knew she was alright?"

"Yes. She was the bait to lure him out. I knew he'd have to tie up his loose ends." Chase takes over, cuffing Roger on top of the tape. "You made a big mistake, bud. I warned you and your sister at lunch. Juniper is my best friend. You should have listened."

Eddie Silver appears in the doorway. As soon as Chase hands Roger off, he waves at someone behind him. Em comes barreling through and tackles me with a hug. "You just couldn't help yourself, could you?"

"Hey, he came to me!"

Chase comes back in, giving me an appraising look.

"I'm not going to a hospital."

"In that case," he says, pulling out his tiny cop notepad. My laugh is fast and harsh. "Can I ask you a couple of questions about the typewriter you sold to a Mr. Lawrence Gilroy?"

"Who?"

The noise of the panic button stops, mercifully, but only in time to hear the grinding, squeaking sound that I can't find. The way everyone freezes and puts their hands out, at least I know it's not all in my head.

Chase grabs me and Em and drags us out of the house. Carmen herds the cats out behind us.

"Juniper, how long has it been doing that?"

"What?"

"That sound?" He points to the shop. "Your building is not safe." He ducks as if the whole thing is going to topple at any moment.

"A few weeks, I think."

He pulls me farther away, and we end up at his patrol car on the street. I look around at all the commotion, three cop cars, an ambulance, and Ms. Minnie's face glued to her window.

"Mr. Gilroy," Chase continues, unfazed by any of it. "You sold him that typewriter that used to sit by the door, right?"

"Aww, you recognize my typewriters?"

"He's dead."

Epilogue

Sunday

The cats are finally used to Em's house, our new house for the time being. Turns out, building an entire office in an unfinished basement of an old building, complete with new doors, and not consulting an engineer, is a lot more dangerous than one might think. It's gonna be a while before we're back in our tiny little apartment. For now, I suppose we can handle having Em's whole house as our new playground.

And she even has an office for me, here. Go figure.

The only thing I have to get used to is her incessant need to 'entertain.' This is the third night this week we've had company over. This time, it's the entire gang.

Jasper and Maura sit at the far end of the dining room table, for which I'm thankful. Beside them are Chase and Becky. I can't wait to bend her ear about the Adairs and what all has happened since Roger and Francine were arrested.

Finally, Em and Eddie sit on either side of me, making lovey faces at each other. So gross.

I'm the only one here not paired off, and that's totally fine by me. It's also why I get to sit at the head of the table like a mob boss.

Jasper holds up his glass of water. "Cheers to Irons and Caine Investigations for their first official win!"

Chase holds his water up to clank glasses. "Congrats! But does it count if you aren't getting paid?"

"TBD," Jasper says, causing Chase and I both the raise an eyebrow.

Becky holds up her glass. "I'm glad what's left of that family is going away for a long time. I only wish it could've happened sooner. All those poor people. And to think I worked for those two."

Everyone else raises their glass for the toast. I point mine at Becky specifically. "Hey, if you hadn't worked for them, I never would have gotten the desk."

Jasper adds, "Yeah, and the ledger never would-"

"Diary!" I snap. He's been trying to adopt Roger's awful name for the diary and I won't let him.

With a heavy sigh, he says, "The *diary* never would have been found. And this case might not have been closed."

"That's for sure," Chase adds. "There was so much stuff in that diary that can and will be used against those two in court. Wonder if their sibling rivalry will include who gets the longer prison sentence?"

Speaking of siblings, I send a group selfie to Lys and Ry, then one of just myself at the head of Em's table. 'Can't wait to see you at the reunion!'

The dinner settles into quiet chatter between couples and the clanking of forks. But my mind isn't settled. This is the last thing I want to be thinking of right now, but Chase's words about what was in the diary have me concerned.

If I'd not turned over the diary, would we have been able to solve the case sooner? What did I miss by not having the middle section? Did Carmen's grandmother fall victim to the Adairs because I gave up a clue?

Em places a hand gently over mine. "You did a great job."

I smile and squeeze her hand back.

"Now what?" She gestures down the table at Jasper. "Irons and Caine sounds legit. You ready to take on paying clients?"

I don't know. Am I?

Yes!

My mind reels with all the possibilities. I'm almost done with my course. We started our self-defense class, finally. Next time someone tries to attack me, I'll be better prepared.

"Well, I feel confident we solved the case of who murdered Mrs. Adair. I don't know why I'm still surprised when it turns out to be someone in the family. But I don't know if I'm ready to take on more clients. There's still-"

Em nods. "Still so many unanswered questions."

I can't help but smile. "I know! Isn't it great?"

Also by

Murder in the Gallery: A Gallery Café Mystery
Book 1 in the series
An art gallery cafe, a dream, and.....murder.

Lola has been working in the Gallery Cafe for her Uncle Iggy for a long time. She loves working in this business and dreams that she will one day be able to take it over from her Uncle. The small town of Fawnwood is the perfect location for this quaint bit of art and coffee. Lola loves working for her Uncle. She made arrangements with him to allow her best friend, Polly, to display some of her own artwork. When Uncle Iggy turns up dead, it turns the town upside down. Everyone loved Uncle Iggy, or so they say. Lola didn't want to take over the business like this, but this murder meant that someone was trying to take over the gallery.

Investigating with Polly and with the help of Tetley, her pet rabbit, Lola uncovers old secrets, and unexpected suspects, which could put all their lives in danger.

The Art of Murder: Mysteries from the Antique Store
Book 1 in the Series
A new antique store, a new painting, and Old Man Foster falling off of the roof.

Juniper had bought the old craft store from Mrs. Horwitz and was nearly ready to open her very own antique store. Junie was always on the lookout for old and unique antiques. Mr. Fluffster and Spot enjoy running around the store, but they especially enjoy their new sleeping spot on the 18th century chaise lounge.

At the funeral of Old Man Foster, high school friend, now Sheriff, Chase Adler reveals that his death may not have been an accident.

Growing up, Juniper had always been afraid of Old Man Foster, thinking he was mean and scary. He lived alone in that big old house on the hill. Juniper kind of felt guilty about that now, that's why she bought that painting during the estate sale, and because it would look good in the new store.

After the painting gets stolen, Juniper and best friend Emerald, with help from Mr. Fluffster and Spot, are compelled to find out what did happen to Old Man Foster, and along the way they uncover secrets no one wanted to get out that brings danger to anyone snooping around.

Murder in the Hidden Room
Book 1 in the Series

Veronica Woodworth left her estate to her granddaughter, Elsie, when she passed away. Now, with the money from the inheritance, Elsie could open her very own flower shop. Her best friend, Dayton, thought the manor guest house would make the perfect bed-and-breakfast.

Soon after they arrived, the house cat led Elsie right to the missing butler, murdered. All cats could be weird sometimes, but Florent seemed to be weird most of the time. Florent led Elsie straight to a hidden room in the kitchen and even helped her figure out how to open the door. In all of her time playing in the manor, she never knew this room was here. But someone did.

Following clues that sometimes led in circles, Elsie, Dayton, and Florence stumbled upon secrets that the killer did not want revealed and could have led him or her to kill again to cover the tracks.

Lunchtime Murder: A Food Truck for Hire Cozy Mystery
Book 1, more coming soon.

Welcome to Little Brooke, Oregon, a quaint, quiet town surrounded by local shops and boutiques, and all year round. The Food Truck Circle sits parked in the middle of it all.

Ginger is giddy with excitement to now be a member of the Food Truck Circle. It makes her feel like a part of something important. After leaving dinner at her mother's house, Ginger returns to her truck to retrieve her lost house keys. But she finds something wrong, terribly wrong.

Her truck has been moved from its original spot and a person lay murdered under the wheel of her tire.

The investigation heats up. Ginger is the prime suspect.

With the help of her new pup, Porkchop, she must race against the clock to find the true murderer. If not, the town may have to cancel the annual "Best Buttered" Food Festival, the best festival in the county. The Food Truck Circle is the best-smelling part of town and people who might normally pass through a small, insignificant town like Little Brook now stop specifically for their Food Truck Circle treats, at least until now.

About the author

My name is Sydney Tate. I have lived in North Carolina my entire life, but I have been all over the state. I was born outside of Charlotte, moved to the mountains as a child and my first teaching job took me to the Marine Corps Base in Jacksonville, so I was very close to the ocean. I have been a special education teacher for more that 27 years, a job I love and am passionate about. I currently live with my son, 3 cats, and a very large dog.

It doesn't seem like I get any free time, but when I do, I enjoy working in the yard, hiking, camping, kayaking, easy mountain biking, playing card and board games, and spending time with family and friends. I enjoy watching football and hockey. I love all types of books, but my favorites are Cozy Mystery and fantasy novels. My favorite book series being Lord of the Rings. Some of my other favorite authors are Terry Brooks, C. S. Lewis, Sue Grafton, and Rita Mae Brown.

I enjoy reading Cozy Mystery and one day I had an inspiration, "Write some of your own". I have very much enjoyed being the author of these books. It is/can be a lot of work, but it is also fun for me. Until

I started publishing my own books, I never realized how much more goes into it beyond actually writing.

I also never realized before how important reviews are to your work. We see 'review this and review that' all the time. In the past, I left a review sometimes, and well, most times I didn't. Now, I will be sure to leave reviews whenever I can. I would very much like for you to consider leaving a review for this book, or any of my books that you have read. I do read the reviews on Amazon, Goodreads, and Bookbub. I get lifted up by many and while some don't necessarily give me a lift, they most of the time have good comments, thoughts, and suggestions. If you have left, or will leave a review, I thank you.

I do hope that you will continue reading my books, and first and foremost, I hope you enjoyed the read.

Best,

Sydney

Made in United States
Troutdale, OR
02/27/2024